Bangkok Rules

by

Harlan Wolff

Copyright © 2012 Harlan Wolff

ISBN 978-1-62620-586-4

Edition 2013
Published by Bangkok Ink

Author email: harlanwolff@hush.com

Printed in Thailand by Kijpaisarn Printing
kjp.publish@gmail.com

This is a work of fiction. Names, characters, places, and incidents either are the product of the author's imagination or are used fictitiously. Any resemblance to actual persons, living or dead, events, or locales is entirely coincidental.

Cover Design by Esau Boen

"We serial killers are your sons, we are your husbands, and we are everywhere. And there will be more of your children dead tomorrow." - Theodore 'Ted' Bundy

PROLOGUE

Valkyries filled the inside of his car and hung around the outside like a loud mist. He had reconfirmed his status as a god so he was attentively listening to every glorious note of Wagner at full volume. Only Wagner was powerful enough and had sufficient metaphysical depth for the ears of gods whilst instilling the necessary terror in mortals.

His shiny new black Mercedes raced and bounced along the potholed dirt road raising a cloud of dust in its wake. The old man didn't usually have a heavy foot but he was annoyingly late and the sun's rise was imminent. He cursed the poor farmers who were out walking to their fields at such an inconvenient and ungodly hour. He was getting careless in his old age. He had never cut it so fine before and he sure as hell was never going to leave it so late again. He had no choice but tolerate the dirt and the gravel that was kicked up by his wheels as they spun for traction. The small stones would leave marks on the perfectly waxed paint and he wasn't happy about that. The Mercedes was his pride and joy.

He had driven off the highway somewhere past the ancient capital of Ayuddhaya. He wasn't totally sure where he was but he knew how to get back to the main road, which was all that mattered. He drove with his back ramrod straight and his face pushed forward so his eyes could see through the tiny gaps in the red fog of laterite dust. He identified a dirt lane to his left that ran beside a dry irrigation ditch to a field that looked neglected and not farmed. This would have to do, so he turned left and drove a couple of hundred meters until he couldn't see anyone in his rear-view mirror. He stopped the car beside the ditch. His breathing was fast and he could feel his heart beating. He lived for this.

He went to the back of the car and opened the boot. She was perfect, he thought, and now she was his forever, nobody else could ever have her. She looked young, she might well have been. It was hard to tell with Thai women. From the neck up she was without blemish. The perfect long, shiny black hair covered the bloody stumps where her ears had been and she had retained the face of an angel. From the neck down the naked broken and slashed torso was covered in blood and gore. My god you are beautiful, he thought as he hurriedly lifted her small body out of the plastic and duct tape lined boot. He carried her into the ditch for the ritual of cleaning, and gently laid her down on a bed of brown leaves.

Then, with agility that belied his years, he jumped from the ditch and retrieved a plastic supermarket bag from the bloody boot. He hastily took several beer bottles out of the bag and removed their plastic caps. From the bottles he poured petrol from one end of the body to the other. Normally, he wouldn't have rushed but today was different. He grabbed a newspaper from the front seat, rolled it up, lit it with a match, and dropped it into the ditch without ceremony.

When the police eventually responded to the phone calls and arrived at the scene, the local farmers were gathered around the blackened smoking remains still taking pictures with their hand-me-down telephones held together with sticky tape, glue and brightly coloured rubber bands. All the farmers could claim to have seen was a cloud of dust moving fast away from them towards the main highway to Bangkok.

One smiling, gap toothed, leather faced local villager on a rusty bicycle told the cops that he was sure the vehicle had been a very new S class Mercedes driven by an elderly foreigner and sounding like it was full of screaming ghosts.

Harlan Wolff

The police called him a fool and disregarded his statement as the uneducated ramblings of a village idiot. Everybody knew that elderly foreigners with ridiculously expensive cars didn't dispose of bodies in rural Thailand at five o'clock in the morning.

"The demons were protecting me. I had nothing to fear from the police." - David Berkowitz

CHAPTER 1

It had been another monsoon Monday and Sukhumvit Road, the neon artery of boozy expatriate life, was knee deep in foul-smelling water. Carl Engel, Bangkok's longest suffering private investigator, had taken shelter from the storm in a side street, his car parked a short distance from the main road. He had gone seven weeks without a client and had been forced to sell a hand-carved ivory chess set from Hong Kong that had been given to him by his long dead father. The sale had provided him with enough cash flow to last a couple of months and temporarily alleviated his fear of poverty. Being broke was the only thing that Carl was still scared of. Death had tapped him on the shoulder enough times for him to develop a certain level of immunity but Bangkok was no place for a foreigner to be penniless.

He had left home early and had been lucky not to break down and get trapped in the rising water. This he interpreted as a reward for putting aside his usual pessimism and embracing the possibility of turning the day's unexpected potential client, an endangered species, into a badly needed cash injection. The early start had left him with time to kill and growing impatience for his appointment with his latest opportunity. Glaring at the clock on the wall was not making the hands move any faster so he stopped but soon found himself looking at his watch instead.

The floodwater had reached the bottom of the doors on his classic 1977 red Porsche, an impractical car at the best of times. It was over thirty years old and impossible during the monsoon season. Women had come and gone in his life but the car had stayed. He was looking at the old Porsche through the window of Duke's American Bar and Restaurant, one of the few places that opened early enough for breakfast. The rain had been heavy, not cats and dogs, more like elephants and buffaloes. Fortunately Duke's entrance was high enough to keep the water at bay. Whatever happened outside, things inside would carry on as usual and in case of emergency there was a guesthouse with a few cheap rooms upstairs.

Carl had once lived in the guesthouse and

called Duke's home for a few months following the implosion of one of his marriages - a period of loose women, poker and binge drinking, which had come to an abrupt end when the cards ran cold and his money ran out. This was followed by some introspection that had all the comfort of going down a sewer in a glass bottom boat followed by a good scrub and brush up as he rejoined the world of making money as opposed to spending it.

Carl Engel's dark hair was peppered with grey. He was above medium height and slightly over medium build. His belly had grown with every year since his fortieth birthday so he had a decade of growth to contend with. His height helped him to carry the extra weight but now that he had hit fifty the belly was starting to take charge.

He liked expensive Italian clothes but wasn't flashy. That day he wore jeans, a black polo shirt and a grey linen sports jacket that wrinkled with wear. To complete the look, he wore soft black leather driving moccasins with no socks. On his wrist he wore a Girard-Perregaux chronograph. It was a valuable timepiece that had somehow avoided the pawnshop and stayed on his wrist through thick and thin. He chose to look chic and successful to camouflage the tidal nature of his finances. His face looked thoroughly lived in but he had always maintained the spark of the undefeated in his pale blue eyes.

In his youth Carl had been fortunate enough

to experience all Thailand had to offer. Once upon a time he'd even been an idealistic romantic but his work had quickly put an end to that. Carl had seen the best and the worst of people, mostly the worst. Through experience he had reached the conclusion that nobody ever really knew anybody, as there were always parts that were kept hidden and were exclusively reserved for other people or situations. He could see deeper into people's souls than most and it left him with no doubt of the duality that existed below the surface. Carl had come to believe that romance required putting someone on a pedestal and he could no longer do that.

He had over thirty years of history with Duke's American Bar and Restaurant and liked to drop in from time to time for a shot of nostalgia. The customers Carl had known over the years had come and gone. Some of them had left dead and some had left by airplane. Fading eight by ten photographs of a youthful Carl with some of them lined the walls. He had always thought it fortunate that very few people looked at the pictures of his youthful smiling and overtly optimistic face standing beside the long departed. Funny thing about the dead; he still expected them to walk through the door one day. The ones that had left by plane would eventually walk through the door. Bangkok had that effect on people. They always came back.

Carl was sitting alone at a round table that had

wooden chairs for eight people. It had started life as a poker table that had taken pride of place in a Patpong go-go bar run by Texans with ten-gallon hats. Poker was illegal as was all gambling not in the hands of the government so the owners would send the bikini clad girls home, lock the doors at 1 a.m. and play cards until the sun came up. The table's history went all the way back to the Vietnam War era and had seen a lot of money change hands over the years. When the go-go bar finally closed its doors following the death of the alcoholic owner, the legendary piece of furniture had somehow made its way across town and become a dining table in Duke's. Carl liked the table.

Two men standing at the bar were looking in the direction of the window and laughing like schoolboys. They were Tom and Gary Downing, known around town as the Drowning brothers because they had made their fortune building and maintaining swimming pools. They were an expatriate success story and Carl had always been partial to a happy ending.

"Hey Carl," the larger of the two brothers called out. "You know how you do all that undercover stuff? Fixing things and investigating and so on?"

Carl looked up without saying anything.

"We just really want to know something. How do you do all that in a bright red Porsche?"

He knew they were trying to be funny, rather

than insulting. He had tracked down the location of a victim held by a highly unpleasant group of foreign gangsters and local Thai police. The gang had kidnapped and tortured the friend of the smaller quieter brother and demanded a million dollars ransom. Carl had been hired to investigate the gang and liaise with local police, which was not without personal danger, as the police typically protected their own.

Carl managed the problem by providing large cash incentives to policemen who were not related to the perpetrators and then feeding the police information he got from working the streets. They found the gang in four days and got the victim back without having to pay any ransom. Carl had managed the ransom negotiations using an alias and bought the police the time they needed to apply for the court warrants and permissions necessary for kicking down the doors that were required for Carl's plan to work.

A thirty-man metropolitan police commando unit carried out the rescue. The commandos blew off the doors of the townhouse where the victim was being held and went in with guns and stun grenades. It had been a big story. Although Carl had made sure he had not been mentioned in the tabloids, the client knew he had put everything together. Carl knew he knew because he had happily paid Carl's enormous bill. The police got all the credit, and the client and the victim's family were sworn to secrecy. Carl liked to stay in the shadows. It would not be healthy to do what he did otherwise.

"You two are starting even earlier than usual. Do your wives know you have escaped?" Carl asked when their laughter had ceased.

"What else is there to do on a rainy day in Bangkok? Join us for a drink?" the big man asked Carl.

"You have to be joking. Last time I drank with you the beer was spiked with vodka and I went to my now ex-wife's birthday party on rubber legs. It's a little early for me anyway."

"I forgot you don't like to drink when you are leaping over tall buildings in a single bound and wearing your underpants outside your trousers. Anything interesting going on?" the small man asked, assuming that Carl's life was all high voltage.

"I'm not involved in anything at present, I just don't feel like drinking."

"You are not as much fun as you used to be," the smaller man said.

"Who is?" Carl replied.

They mumbled and went back to their breakfast beers. The brothers were fundamentally decent and Carl liked them both, even though they were prone to playing annoying schoolboy pranks on everybody they knew. Carl was left pondering the island that was his car, and wondered where advertising stopped and vanity started. Mind you, it made a lovely noise when it was dry.

"Better you let them buy you a drink. You're much nicer when you are drunk," Pet told him.

Pet was in a foul mood. Her name meant duck and she was his waitress that morning. She had taken a shine to him years earlier and was very angry that her feelings were not reciprocated. In her childlike innocence she could not see beyond her own idyllic vision and begrudged Carl his own interpretation of the future, and whatever else caused him to withhold service. She was clearly the extremely possessive type but Carl had already lived in that nightmare. He wanted to tell her that she shouldn't hold a candle if she didn't know where it had been, but some things just couldn't be translated.

"Why do you read the menu? You always order the breakfast," she said to him in Thai as she took the menu from his hand and turned on her heels and waddled away.

She returned with his order ten minutes later and slammed it angrily in front of him. If they'd been married and he had come home the previous night drunk and covered with lipstick her behaviour wouldn't have been any different.

There had been a drunken night once when he had almost given her cause to have a claim on him. She had cupid lips and her body was willing, firm, brown and cuddly. He thanked God that he had found a moment of clarity and been able to resist her seductive charms. The picture of Carl and Duck Engel that he had was very different to her vision. The other reason was she had the look of a bunny boiler in her sweet eyes.

Carl wondered what she saw in him. He was fifty, ten kilos overweight, and wearing heavy black reading glasses. Women must like ugly men, he concluded, as he was more popular now than he had been when he had been in his twenties. Carl had tried harder in those days, and he had even briefly been overtly romantic. He had become a retired romantic since he had learned the cost involved. She hovered nearby in case he changed his mind.

The doors flew open and Bart Barrows made his less than sober entrance. Soaked through from the rain he trudged to the bar in his baggy shorts and squelching training shoes that could only be bought from the bottom shelf at Walmart.

"Beer!" he demanded loudly.

He didn't have to name the brand. The bartender knew what he drank. Heineken bottle in hand, he sat opposite Carl at the round table. Bart Barrows was rotund, unkempt and always angry. He had come from Arkansas to Thailand via the war in Vietnam. A grunt that thought he should have ruled the world, a confrontational American in a non-confrontational Thai world.

"Carl, I have been looking for you everywhere," he half-shouted across the big table as he dripped water into puddles on the floor.

He looked even more dishevelled than usual. Carl guessed he was wearing his gardening clothes. It appeared he had put them on to wade through the floodwater in the rain. This told Carl that Bart had left his house in the morning and had not been out all night. But why would he have left home in the rain when everybody else would have been running for shelter?

"You look like shit," Carl told him.

"Haven't slept at all. It's my daughter, god dammit!"

"Explain," Carl told him sharply, expecting this was going to be pro bono as people that knew him assumed that all assistance should be free. It made him want to send them copies of his alimony bills.

"She has this boyfriend, Thai boy. She is very secretive and I have no idea who he is, or what they get up to. She didn't come home last night. These student murders, I mean, it could be him. He could be the killer. The boyfriend dammit! I need you to find her."

"I am sure she is fine and will be home soon."

"There, look there."

He had thrown the newspaper across the table. He was an angry bully. The newspaper ran a story of yet another young female victim of murder, torture, and sexual violence.

Bangkok was not famous for serial killers but

they finally had one. They called him The Bangkok Angel Killer and the authorities were said to be clueless. The victims were young and female. They had all suffered hours or days of torture prior to death. Their mutilated young bodies had often been found burned beside rice fields a long way from Bangkok. The paper described sadistic rituals involving missing ears, knife cuts and trauma to joints. It also alluded to the possible involvement of local black magic. Thailand had never had such a case as far as Carl knew, not since he had been reading the local newspapers anyway.

"Did your daughter go out with her boyfriend last night?" Carl asked him.

"Yes," he replied, "about eight o'clock."

"Then go home and get some sleep. I'm certain she'll come home sooner or later."

"How the hell can you know that? What, you think I can't pay you?" He was spluttering and getting angry.

"Not that. I'm just certain that her boyfriend's not the serial killer."

"How the hell can you know that?" He was starting to get loud.

"Because this devil is definitely an older man, probably foreign. The FBI would classify him as a type IV killer, the worst kind and difficult to catch. A type IV serial killer has no remorse, doesn't understand the concept. He has what they call an anger-excitation profile. The whole process he performs is his own way to sexual gratification. This man kills for sport. He's not out of control, quite the opposite in fact. Most importantly, in regard to your daughter's safety, the rules of his game are that he must murder strangers. He doesn't kill people he knows. So if your daughter's with people she knows then she cannot be with the killer."

He looked at Carl as if the detective were completely mad. It was something Carl had long grown used to.

"Go home," Carl told him. "Keep trying to call her mobile. Everything's going to be all right." He put on his firm 'this meeting is over' face.

"Damn kids! No respect, acting like whores. Just my motherfuckin' luck for knowing the laziest PI in the whole of South-east Asia," Bart said as he got up.

He paid his bill with wet notes and left noisily. Carl could hear him splashing his way up the street. He did feel sorry for Bart. He was genuinely upset and confused by his loss of control over his child. The one Carl felt really sorry for, though, was his daughter. If Bart Barrows had been Carl's father he wouldn't have wanted to come home either.

Carl finished his coffee and started on the breakfast. A large cooked breakfast with real coffee made from coffee beans was one of the few things that made Carl momentarily forget where he was. However, he was rarely up in time and had no intention of making it a regular event. He only got up before noon when he had a big case and that didn't happen often enough to become habit forming.

Carl took his time eating his breakfast: he had once walked Sukhumvit Road for three days without any food due to lack of funds and although that had been a long time ago, such memories linger. He had weighed sixty kilos in those days and could easily have qualified for a job on the Burma railway. Had he been offered a job laying railway track in the jungle between Thailand and Burma for Japanese psychopaths he would have probably taken it, times being what they were. Carl had put on thirty kilos since his really hungry years, which at the very least gave him the air of being wealthy. He read the paper for a while and then paid the bill and said goodbye to the dark smouldering waitress and the Drowning brothers. They wished him a good day; the waitress didn't.

Carl stood outside and surveyed the flood. It was still slightly above knee deep and the murky water was not going anywhere for a while. He was going to have to leave the car and pull up his trouser legs. He had received a call on Sunday afternoon. Someone needed help and was Carl available? That immediately made him a very potential client. The best clients don't ask the cost on the phone, they are quite rare and not to be taken lightly. Carl never knew how long he might

17

have to wait for the next one. So he needed to go and listen to a story and to do that he was going to get wet.

Carl rolled up his trouser legs and found a taxi that, for a fare higher than for a run to the Cambodian border, would take him where he was going. He was going to arrive a little damp but mostly presentable. He ran a mental checklist and concluded that he was prepared for the meeting.

The taxi's radio was tuned to one of the local news channels. Saturday had brought a coup at sunrise. The tanks had rolled into Bangkok in the early hours passing the old airport to the north of the city, as they always did. The morning television had been martial music and generals, admirals, air marshals and police chiefs displaying crisp uniforms and chests full of medals. Carl wondered, as he did during every coup, what all the medals were for; there hadn't been a war. Maybe they got them for showing up on time to the previous coup.

By Sunday the military coup had made the front page of newspapers around the world and Carl was explaining long distance that there was no reason for concern. The western media always made it sound like the sky had fallen, but that had never been the case. A coup d'état in Thailand was like a no confidence debate with tanks and had little effect on the general population.

From time to time, Thai people went out on the streets and taunted the army, which was an

18

almost certain way of getting themselves shot at. It was not typically their idea, but mobs in Thailand were easily led. The majority of the population would stay at home for a few days and let the military storm pass. The true effects were felt months later when the political power struggles started. The old politicians smelling a possible election in the air created chaos as leverage to get a cabinet post under a military led 'democratic' government. This was Thailand and they had their own way of doing things.

The program on the crackling taxi's radio was mostly martial music broken up by partisan panel discussions providing justification for the military coup. The general in charge was reported to having said it was unacceptable that certain politicians had been making billions of baht. Carl wondered how much was acceptable but wisely kept the thought to himself. The taxi driver thrilled and amazed that Carl spoke his language, was complaining about the military's action.

After a while Carl asked him, "How does it make you feel that those politicians have so much while you have so little?"

The driver shrugged his shoulders and replied, "Don't you understand that they must have done something good in their previous life to get so much in this one?"

Carl nodded even though he didn't understand and probably never would.

CHAPTER 2

Carl had lived on his wits all of his life. People generally perceived him as sincere, possibly because he tried to be when life didn't get in the way. His greatest asset was the ability to turn their trust into tax-free income. He had to live on something and he was a man of expensive tastes.

The Sukhumvit Grande Hotel, a five-star property, had become an important part of Carl's working life. He used it to run his business from and was there at least two days a week. Carl's clients were more impressed by him receiving VIP treatment in a five-star hotel than they would have been by a small office down a Bangkok backstreet. So, over the years he had befriended the staff and made the hotel his own.

He had been at the hotel a couple of months earlier, before his financial drought, holding a complicated meeting with four police colonels regarding the Thai police's legal interpretation and attitude toward shady foreign businessmen, white collar criminals who were happily paying Carl for the information. Carl was in the middle of the meeting when the hotel manager, Fritz Freysinger, tall, Swiss, dressed like an undertaker, relatively new to Bangkok and antiseptically efficient, showed his disapproval of Carl's influence over the hotel's staff.

It was Carl's own fault there was a conflict. He had been at a cocktail party in the ballroom of the hotel when the manager had come over and introduced a friend from Germany. "I want you to meet my friend Graf Felix Von Gorbitz, he is a real Count." Carl looked him up and down then turned to the manager and said, "Sorry to hear that. I find it commendable that you still put up with him though."

Since that day the manager disapproved of him and the day Carl was talking to the colonels was an opportunity for revenge so the manager came over and said, "Nice office you have here," hoping to expose and embarrass.

"Cheap too!" Carl replied.

He knew exactly what Carl meant. Five people drinking coffee under crystal chandeliers would cost the equivalent of forty American dollars. It was far more impressive and a lot less expensive than paying rent on a proper office. Herr Freysinger's beloved hotel had been called cheap so he chose neutrality and left hurriedly. Carl didn't need him. As long as he tipped the staff well it was his hotel. A hundred baht handed out to a few key people meant he was in control from the car park to the F & B outlets. If the manager didn't like it there wasn't a problem. He wasn't on Carl's list of people to give a hundred baht to and if his sarcasm didn't stop Carl would take him off his Christmas list as well.

Carl rolled down the legs of his jeans, put his shoes back on his wet feet, and looked around the lobby. He liked to make a point of identifying the person he was meeting before they gave out any signals. It took them by surprise and gave him the necessary edge. Carl was looking for the tension that comes from the anticipation of making a confession.

Clients contacted him when something had gone seriously wrong in their life. Something they had tried to deal with but had failed to find a solution to on their own. So, before they discuss a course of action, they feel a need to explain how they got to that point whilst avoiding sounding foolish. Therefore it was a confession. So Carl was looking for someone that was tense and probably more than a little nervous.

Carl spotted him immediately. The potential client looked like an oversized schoolboy sitting outside the headmaster's office. He was at least one hundred and fifty kilos but, like so many foreign visitors to the tropics, he wore shorts and a polo shirt. His belly hung over the belt of his shorts and his huge swollen legs protruded downwards out of the cotton shorts like the creations of a drunken sausage machine. His large cheeks and nose were red from years of drinking and the exertion of breathing in the humid air of the tropics. His hair had receded to leave the top of his head bald but what he had on the sides was left long enough for him to sweep it across the top of his head like a randomly thrown floor rug. He had finished off his artistic creation by dying the hair jet-black. It was not a pretty picture.

Carl thought the man looked like an oversized clown but he had a Rolex watch on his wrist and a diamond ring on his finger so all was not lost. Carl walked over and introduced himself. The man showed his surprise that Carl knew who he was without having been given a description. Carl shrugged his shoulders to give the impression it was merely a magic trick and not to be taken seriously. Carl introduced himself and suggested they move upstairs to the library where it would be more private. They took the ornate stairs in the middle of the lobby.

Carl climbed the stairs slowly so as not to embarrass his whale of a potential client. They eventually reached the library without the fat man needing mouth-to-mouth resuscitation, which was a good thing as Carl had decided that if he collapsed halfway up the stairs he would wait for help and if no help arrived Carl would let him die.

Even Bangkok private investigators have limits to what they will do for a client and this hideous looking fat man was only a potential client.

The client sat his large body in an armchair and after several minutes of heavy breathing he began his story.

"This is a difficult story to tell so I would appreciate it if you don't interrupt. I will answer any questions afterwards." He observed him carefully until Carl nodded his agreement.

"As I intend to be totally honest with you, first I will tell you that my name is Victor Inman and I am sixty-seven years old and my story takes place over several decades. To continue in the spirit of truthfulness I must tell you that there was a time when my brother was quite high up in the CIA. He was posted to Vietnam shortly after that commie cocksucker and friend to the Soviet Union was shot by Lee Oswald in Dallas. No insane conspiracy theory there, my friend. Just a pissed off American alone with his rifle. You do not side with conspiracy theorists I assume. I am counting on you being much more intelligent than that."

Carl assumed he was referring to the assassination of President John F. Kennedy who was no friend of Russia but fortunately, a friendly enough man to have averted World War III. Right wing elements on both sides had taken the world to the brink of nuclear war. Kennedy had refused to be influenced by the warmongers and had fortunately chosen a more tempered solution to the Cuban Missile Crisis. He was one of Carl's favourite historical characters.

The alleged 'lone' assassin Lee Harvey Oswald was an enigma, most certainly a villain, and sometime friend of Russia having taken up residence there after denouncing his US citizenship. He later asked for his passport back and returned to the US with a Russian wife. All visa applications for the wife from communist Russia were apparently processed without hindrance suggesting the support of the State Department. Oswald had certainly crossed paths and had dealings with the CIA during his time in Florida prior to that bloody day in Dallas. Carl had always believed a military coup had taken place to take the White House back from uncooperative civilian hands. Carl had seen a few military coups in his time and he knew what one looked like.

There were three good reasons for Carl to hold his tongue: he had agreed not to interrupt, he didn't like right wing arseholes and had a tendency to get angry around them, and arguing politics was a sure way of walking away from the table with empty pockets. He forced his face to remain expressionless. The fat man saw this as approval and continued.

"In all honesty Lyndon Johnson was what the country needed, a proper president and a good American. Under his administration the CIA were tasked with confronting communism across the globe and my brother was sent to Vietnam. He was immediately put in the Phoenix Program and he served his country honourably."

He stared at Carl to see if he was able to follow the conversation. The Phoenix Program was a CIA-backed operation to control the civilian support of the Viet Cong by use of assassination, imprisonment and torture. Carl had spent enough time drinking in Patpong bars with Vietnam veterans to know what Phoenix was. He nodded his understanding.

A very attractive fair-skinned waitress carried a tray to their table and smiled at Carl and asked him how he was. Carl assured her that he was well and asked after her mother who had recently been in hospital. The client fumbled with the sugar he was spooning into his coffee and drank some water. He was still sweating profusely. Carl told the pretty girl he was pleased her mother was in better health and home from the hospital. She gave him her biggest smile and flirted a little with her lovely brown eyes. Then she turned and walked away. Carl, having affirmed his status at the hotel, gave his attention back to the fat man in front of him so he could continue his story.

"He returned to the US around 1975, shortly after the fall of Saigon. He was lean and physically fit, not a follower of the family love of good food that, in all honesty, as you can see, I am a victim of.

He was married in 1982, and had two children, the usual disaster. He started a real estate company and he lived well. In 1992 he was accused of being a serial killer. Several girls had been murdered around the greater Las Vegas area. The killings were linked by two similarities; the location of the stab wounds, and the fact that all the bodies were found without ears. The most shocking case involved the removal of the nipples and clitoris with a sharp knife. They were later found in the victim's stomach having been forced to eat them whilst still alive. In all honesty I have never believed my brother was this man but the FBI were relentless and their investigation ruined his business and turned his bitch of a wife against him."

He stopped talking and looked away. His distress weighed heavy on his shoulders pulling them forward and downward. This was not a happy man. But so few of Carl's clients were. He looked around the library as if he feared being overheard and then spoke again.

"He came to my house early one Sunday morning, shortly after church. He told me he couldn't take it anymore. He asked me to go to California and befriend homeless people, 'Buy them hooch', he told me. I was to find one that looked as much like him as possible and arrange a meeting. I did this for him and a few weeks later he left Vegas in the middle of the night and I have not seen or heard from him since."

"How can I help you?" Carl asked him in as bland a voice as possible. He had learnt to avoid letting clients think he had an opinion. Carl had an opinion of course. It was his opinion that he was about to make some serious money.

The client fidgeted in his chair before answering.

"To be honest with you my biggest problem was that the killings stopped. After he left there were no more murders. I began to lose my mind and check the news ten times a day hoping a murder had occurred. Anything that would prove to me that it wasn't him. I felt terrible, wishing a horrible death on a young girl just so I could sleep better at night."

He stared at Carl's face to try to see what he was thinking. But Carl had his poker face and wasn't giving anything away.

"Recently our mother died and left us both a lot of money. She also left property that requires our mutual agreement before anything can be done with it. So I desperately need him to come to America or I need a death certificate. I have always suspected that he was living in Thailand as he spent a lot of time here during the Vietnam War. I recently searched for him in the archives of the Thai newspapers online. Instead of finding him what I found was a serial killer with an MO exactly like the one I had read about in the Las Vegas papers twenty years earlier. My brother is now seventy years old so I need to know if he is dead or alive and if he is living in Thailand. Most of all, I need to know if my brother is a murderer. Can you do this for me?"

This was the time to close the deal that would get Carl out of his present financial embarrassment. Most of what Carl did was tedious and for relatively small amounts of money. It paid the bills, just about. But a few times a year he struck gold and this appeared to be one of those times. The trick, Carl knew, was finding the balance between getting as much as possible whilst not scaring the client off.

"Before I answer that I need to ask you some questions," Carl told him.

"Fire away." He was more confident. The talking cure obviously worked.

"I assume you have a picture but it is almost twenty years old?" Carl asked him as he took paper and pen from his pocket and perched some reading glasses on the end of his nose so he could look at the client over the top of them. It was show time and Carl took on the role of the slightly eccentric yet wise detective.

The client took a picture from his pocket and handed it to Carl. A smiling man in his forties with wife and children in the garden of a very upper middle class suburban home. Not the picture of a murderer but Carl already knew that nobody really knows anybody.

"Good, that will help. Did you bring the name of the homeless man? He may not be using that name after all this time, but I will need it anyway."

"James Arthur Peabody was the hobo's name. I have a good memory for names," the client said. Carl listened, then wrote it down and nodded as if it meant something.

"Was there a male in your family that was close to him in appearance?" Carl asked.

"What is the relevance of the question?"

He was showing impatience so Carl knew he needed to take charge.

"Just answer the question please," Carl told him looking at him sternly over the top of his glasses.

"He was said to resemble our paternal grandfather."

"At what age did he die?" Carl asked him still watching him over the lenses.

"Seventy-one."

"Do you have an old family photograph of him a few years before he died?"

"Yes, yes, I can get one sent here." His face was lighting up. Part of the show is allowing the client into the process of playing detective. Delivering their childhood fantasy is included in the fee.

"Tell me anything you can about his activities. Was he a golfer, marathon runner, chess fanatic or anything like that?"

"He played poker. Any kind of poker, he would play anywhere. He was said to be good at it. Whatever that means. Not much else I can think of. He went running every morning, he liked to keep fit." He touched his vast belly self-consciously.

"Did he subscribe to any magazines, clubs, associations or such?"

"Not that I can think of. He did smoke cigars though, big Cuban ones. I once asked him how he got them in the US as they are illegal, but he just smiled and winked at me."

"Poker and cigars," Carl repeated to him as he wrote it down. "Any particular brand of Cuban cigars?"

"Bolivar Churchills were his favourite. There were empty boxes everywhere."

Carl listened and wrote it down. "What about social habits? Did he have lots of friends?"

"Some, but he was more solitary than most people. I believe he occasionally played golf, only for business, not pleasure."

Carl added solitary and golf to his notes. He was running out of questions.

"Can you remember the day he left?"

"It was sometime in July 1992," he answered and Carl wrote it down.

"That should do for now." Carl took his glasses off and put glasses, pen and paper in his pocket. "I will need a running fund of twenty-thousand US dollars deposited in my Singapore bank account. When cases are dangerous or controversial I do not accept payment in Thailand. I will message the bank details to your mobile if you are in agreement with this."

He didn't say no, so Carl continued.

"I will need to grease the wheels of justice to get things done, especially as I will be looking into an active murder investigation. This is not something that I typically agree to do as it is extremely foolish and draws attention to my activities. There are no licensed foreign investigators in Thailand and what I do would be illegal if they actually understood what it was. Unfortunately, seeking information on the progress of their investigation will be necessary in this case. I will need to provide good financial incentives to the police to accomplish this with any level of safety so I will not proceed until I receive this payment."

The fat man nodded, so Carl said, "Should further money be needed you will get a full report and be in a situation to judge whether you are satisfied with the progress of the investigation."

As Carl got up the client said, "Good luck." Which Carl had not heard a client say before, especially one he had just cornered into parting with twenty-thousand dollars. It felt ominous and Carl was uncomfortable. You're not supposed to feel uncomfortable when you have just made a big score.

"I will be in touch as soon as I have something to report," Carl said giving him his 'you are in good hands' look as he got up to leave.

Once in the street Carl sent the phone message with the bank details. Within two days he would know if he had a client. Carl was confident the fat man would send the money. Carl knew things about people. He figured he had a client, what he didn't know was if he had a real case or not.

The client called Carl within an hour to let him know that the money had left his bank account and that he had emailed a copy of the confirmation to the email address on Carl's business card. Carl chose to believe him so he decided to break his own rule about waiting until the money was in his hand and start planning. The story had piqued his interest.

He would not usually take a client's word when money was involved. Payment was never confirmed until it was actually in his bank account. This was a rule to live by, as clients did not only lie about case information. Carl put his cynicism aside and started to plan how he would begin the investigation. He dropped his poker face and smiled as he waded through the water along Sukhumvit Road. It felt good to be out of the financial woods again.

CHAPTER 3

Carl had spent two hours thinking in a bar around the corner from the hotel. The Two Ladies bar was open in the afternoon and seedy enough to dissuade most people from entering. The place smelt of drains and mould with a dash of Thai fish sauce. It was the oldest bar in the infamous red light district known as Soi Cowboy which is a narrow lane connecting the side-road Sukhumvit Soi 23 with the thoroughfare of Soi Asoke.

Cowboy had been a tall slim black American serviceman who had come to Bangkok from Vietnam in the mid-seventies and set up a go-go bar called Loretta's with his first Thai wife. When they fell out he opened his own bar opposite Loretta's called Cowboy's. The street quickly became known as Soi Cowboy. The new name was soon adopted by its customers and by Bangkok's taxi drivers until it stuck. He was charming, loud, irresponsible, and a world-class bullshit artist. He died broke in the 1990s many years after having the street named after him. Cowboy and Carl had drunk a lot of whisky together over the years.

Carl had always found it easier to think in public places. Bars had always been his places of choice for his brainstorming sessions. Carl's investigations began with a hypothesis and then a plan to prove his theory wrong. Carl strongly believed in this method as trying to prove a hypothesis correct is dangerous, as the detective's own theory will decide what he sees. Carl's working hypothesis was that his client was full of shit. All he needed after that was a plan to try and prove that he wasn't.

The Two Ladies Bar was as good a place as any to be alone with his thoughts. Putting on the right attitude and tipping well was essential to his requirements. Unfortunately the customers were not as easy to train as the bar girls. An overly garrulous tourist type had overhead Carl ordering a drink in Thai and tried to start a conversation with him. The tourist defended his exuberance by explaining to Carl that he hadn't been in Bangkok for very long. Then he asked Carl how long he had been in Thailand.

"So long that I tip the girls here not to play with my dick," Carl said coldly.

He was left alone after that. Being the grumpy old Bangkok hand may not be the most sought after reputation but it suited Carl just fine.

The problem he was wrestling with was how to establish if the passport of the homeless man

James Arthur Peabody had been used to enter Thailand in 1992 or 1993. It was a very well kept secret that the immigration department didn't keep information on their computer beyond two years. In Carl's previous cases it had taken one phone call to an immigration policeman that he had a special financial arrangement with to get full details on a person's comings and goings. When they arrived and when they left the country, where they left from and where they went. But what Carl was looking for was almost twenty years old and so the computer was not an option.

He was aware that there was a warehouse somewhere with all the past records in hard copy and he had been told that potentially it was feasible to retrieve information from there. But by Carl's calculations it would require a police case, paperwork between departments, and take several weeks. He didn't have that much time, as he needed to impress the client. Clients needed to be convinced, shown a little magic trick or two. Otherwise they could lose interest and, God forbid, ask for their money back.

It occurred to Carl that he was assuming that the target would not have kept his initial identity, would not have renewed the passport and would not still be traveling on it. Thoroughness would require confirming this.

Carl finished his drink and stepped outside for a cigarette. He had learnt the hard way to never leave a drink on the bar when he was going to the toilet or briefly stepping outside for a cigarette. He would always finish the drink and order another one when he came back. The Two Ladies was safe, they knew him and they wouldn't let a stranger near his drink, but it was a discipline he had learnt the hard way, so he gulped down the remaining liquid.

Opening the door of an air-conditioned bar in the middle of the afternoon was always a thermal shock. The curtain of hot thick air hit him and brought back the memory of the first day when he had stepped off a Bangladesh Airlines DC-8 at Don Muang airport and felt Thailand for the first time. The sign on the wooden hut of the bucket shop at Earl's Court train station in London had said, 'The Cheapest Air Tickets in London'. The sign had caught the eye of the teenage Carl Engel. That was the day he decided to see the world but then never made it further than Bangkok. That had been over thirty years ago and in another lifetime. Carl always drank in the afternoon back then, vodka by the bottle, Stolichnaya if they had it. But, having aged and become less familiar with daytime drinking, the hot air made him feel drowsy.

Carl was pleased to see that the floodwater was already less than a foot deep and would be gone in a few hours. He made the call to his contact at immigration to run a check on recent travels to and from Thailand of US citizen James

Arthur Peabody. Carl finished the cigarette and went back inside the bar in search of his second wind.

The tourist that Carl had driven off earlier came and sat next to him. He tried to order a drink from the girl behind the bar in Thai but failed miserably and reverted unhappily to English. He was obviously drunker than the last time he had spoken to Carl.

"Look," he said slurring, "I ain't wanting to bother you. I just wanna know how to talk Thai like you."

"Why?" Carl asked him.

"Well, see, it's like this. I have this girlfriend and we get on OK but I always had this, like, ambition of speaking to her in her own language."

"And what makes you think if she has nothing to say in your language that she could possibly have something to say in her own?" Carl snapped.

The tourist was turning red and his body had stiffened. He looked like he wanted a fight but obviously thought better of it and moved to a safe distance further inside the bar, near the toilets. Carl didn't have anything against him but he was not in the mood to adopt him and become his tour guide to the Bangkok red light experience. He was getting less tolerant of people with every passing year.

Carl exhibited all the symptoms of Expatriate Bubble. When old Bangkok hands have had enough, they retreat into their anger-powered

Expatriate Bubble where they can control contact with the outside world and avoid being hit by the flying bullshit. In Carl's opinion this was not a healthy way to live but he had ended up there anyway.

The cool and windowless place made him forget that it was a bit early for his drinking habit and he quickly got back in the swing of it. After all, he hadn't actually received payment and so was entitled to take the rest of the day off. After the fifth drink Carl always found an excuse to avoid work. It would be a couple of hours before he expected to be called back by his man inside immigration so he decided that he might as well kill some time and enjoy himself.

An older waitress with a reasonable English vocabulary was talking to an obvious tourist. He was besotted with a young girl with the more voluptuous figure of the new generation that had grown up on dairy products. Foremost company of the US had a plant in Thailand during the Vietnam War making reconstituted milk, yogurt and ice cream under contract to the US military. When the troops pulled out they had no customer base, as most Thais were lactose intolerant. By the 1990s they had weaned the younger Thais onto their products.

The girl was under twenty years old so would have got the full calcium, protein, and cow fat package. It may not have been as healthy as the original Thai diet but it had given her a body by Michelangelo, which was fine by Carl. She was too young for him unfortunately. Children had never been Carl's thing. He still looked though. The love-struck tourist was a bit older than Carl and he seemed to think her age was perfect. She looked bored and disinterested.

The older English-speaking waitress left the amorous barfly and the voluptuous girl together and came over to Carl and said in Thai, "He likes her a lot."

"Who wouldn't? She's very beautiful and very young."

"She is beautiful but still stupid. She's my daughter and I am teaching her to be clever. All she wants is to be with young people but I told her, young people have no money. She'll learn though, I must make sure she learns. She looks up to you. Maybe you can take her for a few days. You could teach her what makes men happy."

"What makes you think I'm happy?"

"You spend lots of money and get drunk a lot."

Then she took the frustration off her face, put on a smile, and walked back over to her daughter.

When the phone rang over two hours later Carl was in alcohol's happy middle phase and surrounded by half-naked women. He was entertaining them with Thai jokes, which are always of a sexual nature. Unfortunately his repertoire was limited and it signalled that it was time for him to leave the party. After having been drunkenly playful and having a dozen or so girls rolling around laughing for half an hour Carl could hardly sit in silence again. So he let the phone ring out while he paid his bill.

As soon as he stepped outside he saw the flood had reduced into a giant puddle. He returned the missed call and got the information he had expected; there was no record of a James Arthur Peabody entering or leaving Thailand at any time in the previous two years. He put the phone back in his pocket and walked through the puddle with his confident and rolling stride, splashing water all around him.

Carl's next stop was a dimly lit bar where all the waitresses were advertised in lace G-strings. 'Brevity is the soul of lingerie' said a sign on the wall. Brevity was taken so seriously that some of the girls didn't bother with underwear at all. The owner was Croatian and had come to Thailand to escape the horrors of the Balkan war. He went north to the hills of Chiang Mai where he chose heroin over his military uniform. Then, after a couple of years, he had chosen lingerie over the heroin and the result was a fetish lounge on Soi Cowboy. Lingerie is a relatively harmless fetish, which is probably why the place was not overly popular.

The owner's name was Oleg. He was behind

the bar hovering near the cashier. He had the hollow cheeks and vague eyes of a person who had abused narcotics to the extreme and somehow lived to tell the tale. Oleg was tall and very thin. He dressed like a teenager in skinny jeans and an overly elaborate shirt and had hair that was spiked up with gel that Carl had always thought looked like a toilet brush. He atypically bought Carl a drink. Oleg never bought anybody a drink.

"Carl, I need your help," he said, with the Balkans still in his accent.

"Do I get a clue Oleg or do I need to guess the problem?"

"You see my bar, it is very quiet, no?"

"Yes Oleg, always quiet."

As they spoke, a heavy red felt curtain that had been drawn across an alcove at the far end of the bar opened. Behind the curtain was a synthetic leather sofa that Oleg's girls used to solicit tips for fellatio sessions. A slightly overweight and dangly breasted girl came out followed by an enormous Russian tourist. The Russian grunted at her in Russian and kissed her on the cheek whilst slipping a thousand baht note into her eager hand. The Russian left hurriedly.

"We serve anybody these days," Oleg said in disgust as the door closed behind the Russian.

"So what can I help you with Oleg?"

"I was wondering after all these years you have been coming to Soi Cowboy if you can give me advice on what to do to make more customers come."

"I hope what you mean is how to attract more customers to the bar. Otherwise it is way outside my field of expertise Oleg."

"I don't understand."

"Never mind, I will tell you a story Oleg. Once upon a time there was a bar on Soi Cowboy and the owner, being new in town, asked a customer for advice. What is wrong with my bar, he asked his only customer of the night? Quite obvious, he was told, you see, the bar is on the wrong side of the room so when the door opens you cannot see the bar or the customers, and as you know, nobody wants to enter an empty bar. The bar owner took this to heart and shut the place down for a month and had the bar demolished and moved from one side of the building to the other. A few weeks after reopening there was little improvement in the number of customers. One night he asked a customer what he thought the problem was. Obvious, he said, the bar is on the wrong side. What do you mean, he demanded? I mean, when the door opens you can see everybody at the bar and what they are all doing and who wants to be seen by people from the street in such a bar."

"I don't get it," Oleg told Carl.

"You will Oleg, you are already halfway there."

Oleg went back to his corner at the other end of the dimly lit bar where his computer was situated. Due to his history with heroin he didn't trust himself with alcohol so was addicted to Coca Cola and the Internet instead. Carl had seen him once sitting at his computer surfing Internet porn sites. Carl had thought this very curious indeed because while Oleg was glued to his computer screen three of his naked girls were putting on a show for a customer with a fat wallet. The show included hot dripping candle wax, spanking, and several dildos. Carl had wondered what Oleg could possibly be captivated by on an Internet porn site while all that was going on but he had decided that he didn't want to know.

The door opened bringing daylight. Damien Southerby came in and sat beside Carl. Carl knew that his real name was Keith Smith but pretended that he didn't. It was better that way. In Bangkok if he wanted to be called Damien Southerby he would get it and that was fine by Carl. He wore a starched business shirt with twinkling diamond cufflinks and a bright yellow Zegna tie. His watch was a gold Rolex also covered in diamonds. Damien had perfectly styled hair, manicured fingernails and the clear skin of somebody who eats well and visits his health club regularly.

Damien was a crook and a very successful one. He sold dodgy foreign currency investments over the phone that guaranteed a large profit to unsuspecting Australians. The gullible Australian investors never had a chance of seeing any of their

together soon," Damien said as he moved down the bar and slipped behind the red curtain to make a deposit.

There wouldn't be a dinner invitation. Carl made Damien nervous and he would avoid Carl until somebody made him more nervous and he needed him again. Damien or as his mum called him, Keith, had bought his own bullshit and saw himself as a successful globetrotting entrepreneur. The white-collar criminals were a funny lot and they were very prone to fantasy. Carl didn't question or interfere with Damien's movie star fantasy world; the envelope was always fat and cash was always preferable. Carl decided to leave the bar before the grunting from behind the curtain started.

By that evening Carl was sitting in one of the crowded big, new and shiny bars that were gradually taking over the limited real estate in Soi Cowboy. He was watching the topless dancers and he was deep in thought. He hadn't intended to get drunk but it never started with that as his plan. In Carl's vast experience, the kind of bars he had chosen to drink in on that day always provided that end result.

As usual, it had taken getting completely drunk to hit the inspiration he required. He would go and see the Dutchman. That was it! The alcohol charged bolt of lightning had struck. Of course! The Dutchman. It was so simple it would never have come to him if he had been sober but without that restraint it had become clear.

The plan would require a lot of luck but investigations typically turned on luck so it was definitely a sound idea. It was time for Carl to go home, sober up, and pay a visit to the Dutchman. He left Soi Cowboy and took a taxi to Duke's to collect his car. The car was dry even if Carl wasn't.

CHAPTER 4

Waking up on Tuesday morning was a shock to Carl's system. It reminded him of why he had been avoiding Soi Cowboy recently. Once he had been the youngest detective in Asia and the bars had been his chosen social life. Then he would drink a bottle of vodka, have wild sex, for a price, with two fit dancing girls and get up the next afternoon full of energy and joie de vivre. Now Carl would wake up alone early in the morning feeling like death warmed up, promise not to drink again, and walk around all day like a pit bull going cold turkey.

Carl fiddled clumsily with the Italian coffee machine and managed to make himself a double espresso without spilling too much of the dark frothy liquid. The strong shot of coffee made his belly rumble and his first cigarette of the day brought on a fit of coughing. A dangerous combination so he climbed the stairs rapidly to the toilet to read a chapter of Churchill's 'A History of the English Speaking Peoples'. Carl had no idea what constipation was and why people complained about it. Thailand had always kept him regular.

Two hours later, shaved and showered – it had taken a while for him to get going – Carl arrived at the Dutchman's house. Carl hadn't called first as the aged hippy didn't have a telephone. But Carl understood his habits well enough to assume he would be home. It was a small house in a medium-sized garden on a lane off a minor street at the suburban end of Sukhumvit Road.

The house was Bangkok old style and had well-matured trees in the garden and a rusty gate at the front. The Dutchman was one of Bangkok's more famous old eccentric expat characters. He dealt antique Tibetan rugs out of his sitting room; that is to say he was mostly broke and in debt. He had been married once and his wife had foolishly tried to make him respectable.

They had established a direct mail advertising business in the late 1980s, his version of going straight. His ex-wife had been a large round woman, Thai-Chinese and madly, passionately in love with money. Her father had been a mister-fixit army major. A lot of plain brown envelopes stuffed with money had been passed to him under Bangkok coffee shop tables. He was known for having a dark side and would, for a fee, happily give somebody a serious talking to including a slap or worse. His daughter had not fallen far from the tree.

Carl knew the marriage was not a happy one when, around 1993, he noticed the Dutchman on Soi Cowboy every Tuesday falling down drunk. After several weeks of this odd behaviour Carl asked him why every Tuesday brought on such self-destructive behaviour? "Because Tuesday is the night Bla-bla-bla wants to sit on my face!" he slurred unhappily.

'Bla-bla-bla' was what he unaffectionately nicknamed his wife whom everybody else politely, and possibly out of fear, called Barbara although that was not her real name. She had chosen it due to an addiction to Barbara Cartland's novels. Carl sympathised with the Dutchman's plight. Bla-bla-bla was not the sort of woman that he could imagine in any sort of intimate situation. There was no surprise when the divorce came soon after that. She had gone away and was living in sin with her money in Vienna. He was down and out in Bangkok. It was hard to say which one of them got the best end of the deal.

The Dutchman's maid 'Pim' came to the gate surrounded by ten yapping small dogs. She smiled when she saw Carl. It had been a while since he had been there last. She liked Carl in the way that women with a need to play mother to an unmanageable rogue are fond of the rogues that they do not have to be responsible for. The Dutchman was her project and the more he argued with her and the less he paid her, the fonder she grew. What Carl saw was a case of full-blown martyrdom, a functional relationship in which the Dutchman was the tantrum-throwing little boy, and she the suffering adult. Carl was confident that they would live happily ever after.

"He's still in bed. Nothing has changed. He is still smoking too much ganja and drinking too much. There is a woman living here, watch out for her she's another one of his whores. She'll be gone soon, like the others. When the money runs out again she will leave." Pim was muttering to herself in Thai as much as to Carl. He had heard it all before.

She opened the door to the house and Carl went in. It was a place he had fond memories of. Everything was old. Even the music collection was vinyl. The house contained piles of antique carpets and the smell of old wood and imported Tibetan dust. The Dutchman lived from hand to mouth even though what he had was highly valuable stock. Deep down he was trying not to sell it, as he'd grown attached to every piece. He always waited until the final demand bills came or the collectors were on his doorstep when it became essential to sell one of his treasured items. It became a matter of timing but time didn't really matter to the Dutchman so he was often in trouble.

"You bloody asshole!" he boomed from halfway down the stairs in pyjamas and bedroom slippers. "Where have you been hiding? I heard your car from up the street. Still driving around like a bloody millionaire then. If you can afford to run that thing you can afford to send out for noodles and beer." He went straight to the open door. "Pim, Pim, get in here, Carl is giving you some money to get beer and noodles. He's hungry."

"You mean you're thirsty," she muttered to him as she bustled into the house carrying a tray laden with coffee cups and water glasses.

Carl gave her five hundred baht and she went off muttering about the annoying habits of drunks and whores.

"So, Dutchman, what's this I hear about you and a new woman in your life?"

"Did Pim call her a whore?"

"No, just muttered a lot."

"You look good," he told Carl sarcastically.

"Rough night," Carl replied as he watched both of his shaky hands negotiating with the hot coffee cup.

"I thought you'd given up drinking like an Arab on his first Asian holiday."

"So did I."

"When you're not completely pissed are you still tilting at windmills, saving damsels in distress and all that nonsense?"

"No, just running errands for Thailand's white collar criminals."

"To hell with them! Let's go to Patpong or Soi Cowboy and get nasty drunk. Meet some naked women and smoke some shit. Just like the old days, just like the old days Carl."

He was at least fifteen years older than Carl but was still living in adult Disneyland. The decades of smoking the coarse Thai marijuana had taken its toll on his lungs. He wheezed when he talked and he wasn't looking good. He was one of the few men standing from the wild times of the Asian hippy trail in the 1970s but it didn't look like it would be for too much longer.

They had become close friends in 1979 when they spent a year together smuggling rubies from Calcutta to Bangkok to defeat India's strict foreign exchange regulations for an Indian moneychanger with an office in Bangkok's Chinatown. It had been a year of high adrenalin including lots of alcohol and Nepali hashish. They both knew that the fact they didn't end up in an Indian jail was more luck than good design.

The partnership had ended at Calcutta airport. The Dutchman had lost his nerve and handed one of the two boarding passes to Carl and run off to go through customs alone leaving Carl to smuggle the rubies. This was against their agreement as they had mutually decided that should they end up in an Indian prison they should not go there alone.

Carl was not concerned that he had several packs of very valuable rubies in his shoes that day as he had successfully carried out several smuggling trips by then. Unfortunately when he showed his passport and boarding pass to the Indian customs officer he was immediately accused of attempting to travel under an assumed name.

The Dutchman had handed him the wrong boarding pass. Carl's name boldly printed on the boarding pass the Dutchman had run off with had obviously not drawn the negative attention that Carl's possession of his had. The Dutchman was happily sitting at the bar inside the departure lounge sipping on a cold Kingfisher beer. Carl's documentation was a different matter entirely. Teenage smugglers were always at greater risk of getting caught.

The angry officers started by accusing him of being in the CIA even though Carl explained that he carried a British passport and that the CIA were in fact an American organisation. The military moustached men in their shiny customs uniforms did not see that as a relevant argument and continued to insist Carl was spying for the Americans.

The entire Calcutta customs department questioned him for forty minutes. He was frisked three times when they ran out of questions. Fortunately they stopped their search at his ankles every time and he had not been asked to remove his shoes. Carl had always been lucky.

Forty minutes later after his insistence that the girl at the airline check-in desk had handed him the wrong boarding pass, they compared the name on his passport with the flight manifest and he was let go. Which was a great relief as the penalties for smuggling gemstones were more severe than for smuggling narcotics.

He had found the Dutchman half drunk at the bar. "What took you so long?" The Dutchman asked Carl casually. Carl didn't answer. He had already decided that his smuggling days were over. Decades later, sitting in the Dutchman's sitting room, Carl found the memory amusing although he hadn't thought so at the time.

"I don't do the daytime drinking thing anymore," Carl told him, ignoring the fact that it was exactly what he had done the day before.

The Dutchman put a vinyl record on his old Technics turntable and lit a joint. Carl recognised it as one of his favourites, 'Monk's Music'. The room filled up with marijuana smoke and the sound of Thelonious Monk's piano. Oh yeah, memories were made of this.

Carl swept away the fog that was taking him back in time. He wasn't a dope smoking gem smuggler anymore. He was a private detective, a serious person handling serious matters. It occurred to Carl that the previous day he hadn't been very serious. Yes, he had picked up a twenty-thousand dollar retainer, which is as serious as it gets, but he was still drunk before the sun went down.

Carl recognised the rising danger. He was on

the verge of attempting to talk himself into something foolish again. That's the problem with nostalgia; the past is always in front of you. But he was not falling for it that day, he decided, and he changed gear into the twenty-first century and declared to himself that the party was at least temporarily over.

"You're well known for never throwing anything away. Do you still have your mailing lists from that direct mail company you ran with your ex-wife?"

"They'll be somewhere in the garage."

Carl knew the Dutchman had never owned a car so the garage had always been his warehouse. "Standard stuff I assume. Sports Club, Polo Club, credit card holders, golf societies, chambers of commerce and such?"

"Yeah, that sort of thing. Why are you asking?"

"I have one of those silly clients. The ones that think life is a movie and they are starring in it. Thinks his wife cheated on him when she was first married to him. Mad as a hatter I'm afraid."

"So why the interest?"

"Someone pays you ten thousand baht for nothing it would be impolite not to take it."

"He gave you ten thousand baht? That's not much."

"Oh, not for a case. Just to find out if the name he heard back then was a real person.

Anyway, if someone gives me ten-thousand baht to come and visit an old friend it seems like a good day to me."

"I suppose it is," he said without a smile.

"So we look at your lists and split the money."

Suddenly the Dutchman was smiling from ear to ear. If Carl could read minds he would have known the Dutchman was making a mental list of all the girlie bars he was going to spend the money in.

"Wait here," he said and shot out the backdoor.

The sounds of Monk and the boys playing 'Well you needn't' from the record player washed over Carl. Don't listen to it Dutchman, he was thinking, yes you need to!

By the time the Dutchman came back the record had finished playing. The Dutchman was bringing endless plastic bags into the house, wheezing with the effort. It took him ten minutes of sweating and puffing before he could speak.

"So what's the name we are looking for?" he asked still out of breath.

"James Peabody, somewhere between 1993 and 1996."

He was pulling out A4 size soft files that resembled manuscripts. They were lists of everything imaginable and most importantly the names were in alphabetical order.

"You start with this lot," he told Carl as he

started making a pile in front of him and another in front of himself.

Pim came back, clanking beer bottles. She brought beer and noodles in on another tray. She had lots of trays. Fortunately the Dutchman was too busy to care whether or not Carl drank his beer so didn't notice that the bottle remained full. The noodles with pork were good and the chilli peppers did wonders for his hangover. They both pushed the empty bowls and chopsticks into the middle of the table and got back to the task ahead.

The first file Carl picked up was marked with big letters on the front, 'The Scandinavian Society'. No chance, but he still went through the Ps diligently. It was never a good idea to give the other person an excuse to be sloppy so Carl made sure the Dutchman saw how carefully he studied the pages. Getting people to the racetrack is one thing but spend too much time patting yourself on the back and they'll never reach the finish line. The next file Carl picked up was a list of subscribers to Bangkok Shuho, a Japanese language newspaper. It was getting ridiculous but he went through it anyway.

An hour later brought the 'eureka' moment. The thinnest file of course, the least likely to succeed, the runt of the litter. It was no more than ten pages.

"What's this?" Carl asked the Dutchman.

"Let me see." He grabbed it from Carl's hand.

He studied it and started laughing.

Carl was in mild shock. There it was, the name he was looking for on a yellowing page, shouting at him from the analogue past. He hadn't expected to find it. It was a case to go through the motions; it's not like he took such an eccentric client seriously. A private detective may start his career with belief in his fellow man but life will get the better of faith and eventually make him cynical. The industry jargon is 'paranoid survival'. Meanwhile, Carl was having a Hollywood moment. Fan-bloody-tastic!

"I had this mistress. The wife never knew," The Dutchman said with a huge grin. "She was cute, from the North, Loei up by the border. Only Thai girl I ever knew with pink nipples. Can you believe it? Pink nipples."

He started rolling a joint from another box, Nepali hashish this time. When he was puffing the pungent smoke he continued. Not smiling but content in that no man's land of a happy memory.

"She worked for a travel company in the business district. A very small travel company, she was the secretary. They organised gambling tours to Macau for rich Thai-Chinese, the kind of people that could lose a million dollars in a weekend without having to commit suicide. The company made most of their real money by arranging cash when the clients gambled themselves broke. The currency control regulations in those days made it almost impossible to get large amounts out of

60

Thailand. The company gave a horrible exchange rate and charged interest, all arranged through our old money changer in Chinatown. It took me forever to get her to make me a copy of their client list but I wasn't going to miss out on having a list of people like that. Last time I sold it was around 1995, to a yacht marina with two million dollar houses for sale. There is a code after the names and information on the back page. Ah, here it is; high stakes poker it says. And here it says a private game on the top floor of the Lisboa casino. Not on public floors, no poker on public floors in those days. Must be rich to have been in a big private game like that."

"What about contact details?" Carl asked him.

"Just an address and phone number."

Just an address and phone number! It was all Carl could do to stay calm. He was having a good day, a special day. Like getting a Christmas card from Easter Island that said Happy Birthday.

"Let me write that down," Carl said reaching for pen and paper while handing the Dutchman five thousand baht with the other hand.

Carl was in a hurry to leave. Not that he felt bad; the Dutchman had got five thousand baht for an hour's work and was more than happy. It would not have been right to tell him the truth. It was necessary for Carl to tell lies for a living but he knew that if it became a lifestyle he would get lost. He understood the fine line between light and darkness because he walked it every day. He liked the light but was drawn to the dark side so he knew that he needed to be careful. Once he let the devil out, the party went on for days. The trouble was Carl liked it.

CHAPTER 5

Carl sent an SMS to the client to remind him he needed the photograph of the grandfather that the target was said to resemble. He also asked for the target's full real name and date of birth. He told the client he could arrange for the picture to be collected from the client's hotel whenever it was convenient.

Carl chose not to mention the morning's findings. He believed that delivering information in bits diluted the magic and invited interference from the client. The purpose of the message was to let the client know that Carl was already on the case and to put his mind at ease.

The client messaged back almost immediately; the picture was being couriered from the US and was expected in a couple of days. The full name of his brother was Anthony Andrew Inman, born 12 March 1943. Carl used his Blackberry to send an email to a contact he had in Las Vegas requesting a full background check on an Anthony Andrew Inman.

The address Carl had got from the Dutchman's records was, by Carl's calculations, somewhere around the middle of Phetchburi Road, which was not far from Sukhumvit, almost as long, running parallel to it. Carl had driven there in the unusually light Bangkok traffic without seeing any evidence of floods or coup. Thailand made him doubt his sanity and memory at times. If these major events really happened why couldn't he see them? Because the veneer was back and the woodworms were asleep.

House numbers in Bangkok were based on a very fuzzy logic and were typically all over the place. Carl fortunately understood the history of how the numbering had been allotted. The confusion had been created when large plots of land had been broken up into smaller pieces and sold. House number one hundred could be a long way from number ninety-nine and there could be dozens of buildings between them, each individually provided with a complex number at different times during Bangkok's rapid growth. Carl functioned well in chaos so he found what he was looking for without too much trouble.

It was a stand-alone building with four floors and a flat roof. The place was deserted and had seen better days. There were unwashed floor to ceiling windows on the front of the building. Carl saw that it was facing the main road but all signs had been removed. Carl concluded that it would have been an office or showroom and not a retail shop. The building was empty and by the look of it had been for some time.

There were eight parking spaces belonging to the building and Carl parked the Porsche in the first one. Beyond the building's private parking area there was a quadrant made up of shop houses operating various businesses and an open area where customers parked. As usual everybody looked. Yes Carl, how do you do it in a bright red Porsche?

There was a rundown noodle shop a few meters inside the quadrant off the main road that had obviously been in business for a long time. One of the few left in central Bangkok. It had become mostly plastic convenience food service in Bangkok but Carl was pleased to see that on Phetchburi Road that was not the case.

Carl went and sat at an old wooden table with a plastic tablecloth displaying its array of condiments, cutlery and toilet tissue. Toilet tissue to wipe your mouth had taken some getting used to until Carl realised that he only considered such tissues to have one purpose because an advertising company in Europe had told him so. In Thailand it was just tissue in a roll which was a far more practical attitude to such things.

Carl ordered an iced tea. He was fond of the Thai black tea, another thing that was becoming extinct because of US cultural products such as the sparkling sugar water that rots your soul. The pungent smell of frying garlic and chilli peppers filled the air. It was how Bangkok was supposed to smell and it made Carl happy in spite of his hangover.

A chubby girl with depression's flat feet that shuffled across the cement floor brought Carl his glass of tea. She would happily move over to Sukhumvit and work behind the counter of a burger joint in an air-conditioned shopping mall. Thailand's worker bees were not a happy lot and who could blame them? Corporations had more interest in them than their own people or their government did and treated them better. Women like her wanted a better life and that would require saluting a corporate logo every morning. She wanted the Orwellian future and the future wasn't pretty.

He studied the place for a while. The restaurant was no longer fashionable but appeared to manage to stay in business due to there being enough low-paid employees in the quadrant who needed to feed themselves on a tight budget.

The old man at a table inside the shop house at the far back was obviously the owner. He was the sole collector of all monies, carried to him by the slow-moving solitary waitress. In the more traditional Thailand the true owner of a business was the one who handled the money. All other ownership structure was purely cosmetic. Carl didn't ask the girl for a bill but walked inside and went directly to the table at the back and paid the old Chinese looking man wearing shorts, vest and flip-flops.

"The tea is wonderful. Much better than that foreign rubbish all the kids drink," Carl told the old man.

"Yes, business is bad now, very bad," he told Carl in Thai with a Chinese accent. He didn't show surprise that this foreigner was speaking to him in Thai.

"I haven't been here for many years. I used to come and eat noodles here all the time. That was fifteen years ago. Everything changes so fast in Bangkok. Great that you are still here."

He didn't show much interest and didn't answer.

"Take that building. It used to provide lots of jobs. Now it's falling apart."

"Big houses for rich people," he said as he fiddled with his abacus.

"So long ago that I can't remember. What was it?"

"Vegas. It was Las Vegas," he told Carl.

Las Vegas Real Estate Company. Their advertisements had been all over town, still were. So this was where they had started. Inman knew the real estate business and liked a bet. Las Vegas Real Estate was not overly creative but was probably an effective name in the Thai market. Carl said thanks to the old man and got back in the car.

The first thing he did once he was comfortable in the air-conditioned car was telephone his lawyer. They had worked a lot of cases together over the years and he was always pleased to hear from Carl.

"Sawasdee Krab Khun Anand, how're you? I am going to SMS you a company name. Can you check the ownership information at the Ministry of Commerce? I am looking for any foreign shareholders. Thanks and same to you. Let's have lunch soon."

Carl sent the name Las Vegas Real Estate Company Limited by SMS to him immediately and drove off. The old telephone number wouldn't be of any use. It was a landline that would have been registered to the building and the building was another of Bangkok's empty shells. One thing about the rundown building that Carl thought was very unusual was that the electricity meter on the concrete pole was still there in plain view and the heavy cables were still connected. What was an abandoned building doing with electricity and who was still paying the bill after all those years?

Carl called Colonel Pornchai, more an academic than a policeman. They had been involved in some serious cases together. He would be able to access social security records from the computer on his desk. Should Inman, alias Peabody, receive any form of taxable income he would be on the computer. But it didn't take Colonel Pornchai long to confirm that he wasn't on any government computer database.

Carl drove through the midday traffic to the Oriental Hotel on the river and walked through the lobby to the cigar shop. There was nobody around and the door was locked so he went back to the car and drove to the Grand Hyatt hotel where they also had a cigar shop. The shop at the Hyatt was busy as it had a private room with comfortable armchairs where customers could smoke. Carl asked for a Bolivar Churchill but was told they were out of stock so he bought a Ramon Allones Robusto instead.

"Do you get much demand for the Bolivar Churchill?" he asked the girl at the desk.

"We don't sell many. They have been out of stock for a while now."

He went into the smoky room and picked a leather armchair. Carl lit his cigar slowly so as not to overheat it. He took a couple of puffs and leaned back. The room was half full of local businessmen, politicians, and a few of the usual rogues. The rogues nodded at Carl and then went back to their whispered conversation. A large man came in and sat in the armchair opposite Carl.

"Heard anything about the coup?" he asked Carl.

"Only that there was one."

The man sitting opposite Carl ran one of the

legitimate stock brokerage companies in Bangkok. He was an elderly English public schoolboy who Carl assumed would have gone to Eton or Harrow. Carl's money was on Harrow as there was a theory about Harrovians wearing brown suede shoes with everything. Today he was wearing a dark blue suit with his well-worn brown suede shoes. His name was Robert Standish and he was a pillar of Bangkok's expatriate society.

"Now come on Carl, we all know you're a spook. Tell me what the gossip is in your secret world."

"But I'm not a spook, I'm merely a struggling consulting detective," Carl told him affectedly as he ceremoniously puffed on his fat cigar. Carl knew that Robert would see denial as confirmation. Bangkok was full of people claiming to be what they weren't, so claiming not to be something often got the opposite assumption. Carl liked the game.

"Very Sherlock Holmes I am sure. But come on old sport, this isn't the time to hide behind cover. You are needed man. So what have you heard?"

"Well Robert, it is like this; over the last twenty years the politicians have started to believe that they are actually running this country. That made them even greedier than usual and instead of discreetly feathering their own nests they tried to claim ownership of the whole forest. So, like naughty children, they got given a red card by the self-appointed referee and sent for an early bath. They are officially suspended for a few matches until they have learnt to behave themselves, or at least found the good manners to invite the referee to play on their team. Nobody likes being left on the sidelines. I don't know when the next game is scheduled but I'm sure they will let us know eventually."

"For God's sake man, this is no time to try and be funny," Robert Standish told Carl in a low shout.

Carl believed that foreigners, particularly the clever ones, didn't understand Thailand because they would not accept its basic venal nature. They felt it an insult to their intelligence to be told that Thailand was not as complex as they imagined. The suggestion that it was simple when they found it so confusing perplexed them. So they chose to keep it enigmatic and inaccessible disregarding its very straightforward foundation of mutual greed and jealousy. To understand Thailand, as a foreigner, the other thing you had to accept was the simple truth that you were completely powerless and your future was in the hands of strangers.

"You know I can't tell you more than that," Carl said in a lower and more serious voice. "You have to read between the lines in the newspaper like everybody else." Carl leant forward, put a serious expression on his face and whispered conspiratorially, "All I can tell you Robert is that everything will be all right. There'll be no changes that will have any dire consequences for you personally, or for your company for that matter." Then Carl put his finger to his lips and said, "Shhhh, your ears only old man."

"Good news then. Thank you Carl. You are sure of this? It comes from a very reliable source then?"

"The highest," Carl said, thinking that it was the most reliable source he could think of, his own opinion. He was usually right though. That and the fact he had Thailand's past history on his side. Thailand's history may not repeat itself but it certainly rhymed.

Robert Standish was pleased. Like many foreigners, he just needed someone to tell him that everything was going to be all right. If Carl had been able to work out how to charge people for going to their offices and telling them that everything was going to be all right he would have made a fortune. There had always been a demand for such a service. Carl just hadn't worked out how to bill for it. Yet.

"Must dash, duty calls," he told Carl as he got up to leave.

"Don't forget that it's all hush hush," Carl told him.

"I won't tell a living soul Carl. Wouldn't want you to get into trouble with the ambassador."

"That's right Robert. Always nice to see you,"

Carl told him as he left.

Carl assumed he was in a hurry to go and tell everybody that Carl the spook said there is nothing to worry about. Lots of people doubt religion but they all believed in Hollywood and James Bond. Carl didn't mind the stories that were made up about him. They were good for business.

Robert Standish didn't care if the streets ran red with blood as long as his beloved stock market stayed healthy. In reality he had little to fear. A few generals rattling their sabres and politicians crying 'freedom' because they had lost control of the money was not a threat to his industry. Both sides of the conflict were stage managed by extremely powerful and wealthy men. These eagles amongst sparrows on both sides were so heavily invested into the market that allowing it to fail was not an option.

The cigar lead had not borne fruit. Carl hadn't expected it to. Luxury retail shops in Thailand are little more than a wonderful advertisement for shopping in Hong Kong's low cost outlets. The lack of demand for Bolivar Churchills in Bangkok suggested to him that his target might still be flying regularly to Macau for his poker habit. Carl wanted to see Macau again and began to see an opportunity to make it happen.

Carl finished his cigar and went looking for somewhere to have lunch. He felt like eating in a restaurant where nobody would know him. He left the car and walked along the Skytrain's public walkway to Paragon shopping centre, the largest shopping complex in Thailand. Carl took the escalators past the high fashion brands from Milan and Paris to the third floor where Bangkok's largest bookshop was located.

He browsed the history section and selected a book about Beirut and paid for it at the counter. Book in hand he took the escalator back down to the first floor and walked over the Skytrain's bridge to Siam Square, the old shopping area. There was a Hard Rock Café there and he assumed that nobody he knew would be there as no self-respecting expat liked to sit with the tourists. The place was full of holidaymakers providing excellent cover and a burger was just what he needed to go with his new book. He could use one hand for the burger and the other hand to hold the book.

CHAPTER 6

Carl went home early afternoon to study his new case and consider his options. His house was a four-story townhouse in a contiguous quadrant of twenty-eight units. The entrance to the complex was a high double wooden gate with a security box and sleepy guard. The security guard was another person on Carl's payroll. Should any unpleasant characters, with or without uniforms, become interested in him the chances were they would befriend and question the security guard. Carl had made sure that he would be told immediately.

On entering the quadrant there was a ground floor visitor's car park area. Each unit also had space for one car in front of their ground-floor kitchen door. The second floor of the complex had a swimming pool surrounded by gardens accessible from all of the units through their sitting rooms. It was designed to be a community area but most residents kept themselves to themselves so it was mostly unused. The swimming pool was where Carl often went to think.

He changed into swimming shorts and took his new book to the pool area. The sun felt good and he was pondering taking a swim. The light was too bright for reading and hurt his eyes. He was feeling relaxed and at peace with the world. Carl had his eyes closed and his face pointed towards the sky. There was a small cough-like sound beside him that made him open his eyes and look around. Not a good thing to do as his face was pointing at the sun. Carl squinted at the tall man standing over him.

"Hello Carl."

It was Carl's favourite neighbour. George Wilde had a habit of sneaking up on him. He had served in a US Special Forces regiment and had spent his youth in the jungles of Vietnam sneaking up on the Viet Cong and now out of habit, he sneaked up on everybody. He was a big man with incredibly large hands and piercing eyes. He was around sixty but remained as fit as he must have been back in his military days. Carl liked him. He had liked his wife too, but she had died in a motorcycle accident the previous month. It had left George undermined.

"How are you?" Carl asked him.

"For someone living with the bonfire of their dreams, not too bad I suppose," he said with his soldier's face.

They sat in silence for a minute. Then looked at Carl again and Carl saw how haunted his face was when he spoke.

"The trouble with life is we spend all of our time waiting for a wonderful moment. The problem is, when that moment arrives we don't embrace it. Instead, we take it for granted and get distracted. Then we promise ourselves that we will get it right the next time and appreciate how valuable it is. That is the human condition, what keeps us going. The belief that there'll always be another chance and this time we won't fuck it up and forget that all joy is fleeting. What makes us carry on regardless of the fact that all life ends in tragedy is the undying belief in tomorrow and the possibility that everything will be all right and the hope that we will know what to do the next time. That's why religion sells. Buy it and everything will work out right in the end. That's their leverage. The hook is that after death everything will somehow get resolved. What nonsense! I am reading a book about archery, Zen and archery actually. It is about staying in the moment, which is an extremely difficult discipline. You should read it."

"I would like that," Carl told him, meaning it.

He liked George and for a while they had laughed all the time. After the ten-wheel-truck had run over his wife's Vespa the laughter had gone and been replaced by dark existentialism. George had lost people during the war but that was different, it had been expected. When he discovered his wife had been squashed by a heavily laden ten-wheel-truck outside an unlicensed construction site not a stone's throw from where he was opening a bottle of wine for their dinner, he went to pieces. The driver had fled the scene leaving empty whisky bottles on the passenger seat and little proof of his identity. George hadn't asked Carl to look for the driver. Revenge was not his thing. The cremation and the weeks that followed it had been emotional. Carl had done what he could.

"Are you interested in some work?" Carl asked, hoping he would want the distraction from his grief. George watched his back when Carl thought a case might get unpleasant and attract the wrong people's attention. It was very comforting to know that he was out there keeping an eye on him. Carl never saw him following him but had never doubted that he was always there watching. George was also useful at meetings when a little extra gravitas was required.

"Shit! You have a big case; you've got your game face on. I missed that. How sordid is this one?"

"Should be routine. Tracking down a man that may be an evil bastard but is nearly seventy so I'm not concerned. He was some big CIA wheel with the Phoenix Program so he may have some ugly friends in uniform here in Thailand."

"You need looking after then. He has a big advantage over you."

"How so?"

"Those guys had no self-doubt whatsoever. You, however, are riddled with it. First thing I liked about you. Yes, my friend. You are right. You will definitely need looking after. I am not going to lose another one." He looked at the water thoughtfully and then continued. "The CIA was a civilian organisation empowered to torture and kill. Being civilians, they chose to prosecute a war against the civilian population of Vietnam. This was deemed expedient as their understanding of military matters was limited and the White House had not adequately supported a military solution by declaration of war. Fighting guerrillas with terror was the strategy of madmen. They gave away the moral high ground and lost us in the military the support of the American people. The entire US military is still hamstrung by that disastrous decision and can no longer take part in a conflict without risking an overly harsh judgment from the people back home. Those warmongering businessmen have a lot to answer for." Then he was gone as quietly as he had arrived.

Carl felt better knowing the oversized ninja would keep an eye on him. George had a look of Clint Eastwood about him and people tended to behave better when he was around. Carl went back to the house to take a shower and see if the email he had asked for had arrived. He couldn't wait to see the man behind Las Vegas Real Estate.

He went upstairs and took a cold shower to

lower the heat on his skin from the strong sun at the pool. The water felt good and cleared the remaining cobwebs from his head. He put on his fisherman's trousers, which were like a sarong with baggy trouser legs, typically made of soft cotton. Around the house he wore them all the time, even slept in them. Carl went downstairs and put Bruch's violin concerto on his old-fashioned tube amplifier with their speakers the size of wardrobes. He selected a medium-sized cigar from a humidor and lit it with a long match. Carl was home.

He sat on the sofa listening to the violin music for a while and then got up and went to his small office off the sitting room. He switched on the computer and waited for it to fire up. Khun Anand, professional as always, had emailed him all the relevant documentation from the Ministry of Commerce regarding Las Vegas Real Estate Co., Ltd. Whenever possible Carl preferred to print everything before he read it. He found it was more tangible when he saw things on paper. His habit was to print everything longer than three paragraphs.

Carl held the printed pages in his hand and he wasn't pleased. The directors, or in this case the director, was Thai and all the shareholders were also Thai. Annoyed, he emailed the police colonel and asked him to retrieve, scan and email copies of their ID card records. He also asked the colonel for the recent travel records in and out of Thailand for the sole director.

This company director was ruining Carl's working hypothesis and he didn't like it. He left his cigar in the ashtray to go out on its own. Havana cigars go out quickly because they are chemical free whilst all other cigars burn evenly like cigarettes. Carl went into the sitting room and let Bruch put him to sleep on the sofa.

When Carl woke it was already evening. The house was silent and he was in total darkness apart from the fine lines of orange light given out by the tubes on top of the amplifier. He checked his phone for messages and found one from the colonel saying he had sent the information to Carl's email address. Carl turned the lights on and went into the office having picked up and relit the cigar. He switched on the computer and started printing the reports and attachments.

The first document he studied was the ID card printout of the managing director. A Somchai Poochokdee aged sixty-nine. The printout showed the face of an old respectable foreigner. Carl had him! The target had used his money and influence to become a Thai citizen. That was how he had solved his problem of arriving on someone else's passport.

He would have had to establish himself as a taxpaying businessman and then after a few years of regularly queuing up at the immigration department would have paid his way to speed up the process of becoming a Thai citizen. It would have taken a few years and he would have had to learn to sing the national anthem. Thus his identity problem would have been solved. He'd become a Thai person and so carried a Thai passport. The name he had chosen was Somchai Poochokdee. 'The ideal man who is lucky' was the best translation Carl could come up with. It was very corny and yet typical of the sort of Thai name people gave themselves when they applied for citizenship.

The next thing Carl looked at was the target's travel record that had been attached to a second email. The airport immigration report showed that Somchai Poochokdee made trips to Macau and a lot of them. He was obviously still in the poker game. Macau had become a Chinese Las Vegas and recently opened several new casinos run by large corporations. There were public poker rooms there now and Carl had heard there was a lot of action at the tables. He took the details from the ID card document and started putting together a plan to meet the curious character in Macau.

A further look in his email inbox showed Carl the usual spam telling him he needed an extra-large penis and a pill to keep it permanently hard. He deleted those first, then he deleted the Nigerian scam mails advising him of an unexpected windfall. That left two unread emails. One was from a woman he had known telling him that she was unhappy and her husband was not treating her as well as she had hoped. The other email was an offer of work performing a character assassination of somebody that the would-be client claimed had annoyed him.

Carl ignored both of these emails, as he saw no point in replying. The first was standard Internet flirting from an old flame. Carl's grandmother had told him never to reheat old romances or dishes containing mushrooms. The second email was from a man trying to buy an attack dog but Carl never chased or fetched sticks.

Then Carl had to do what he had been avoiding. He Google searched the Bangkok murders. Gruesome stories of how several young girls, mostly university students, had left the world. They would have suffered terribly before they died. Whoever perpetrated the crimes was highly skilled in acts of sadism. The final act was always stiletto stab wounds to their lungs through their ribs, causing them to drown in their own blood, followed by the removal of both of their ears. Carl then did a search on the Nevada murders. There was not much there as so much time had passed. However, what he did find was striking in similarities. Also of interest was the fact that authorities had questioned a Tony Inman, real estate broker.

The next thing Carl did was Google search Las Vegas Real Estate, Bangkok. The search revealed a medium-sized company that was active in the market and with an office located on Silom Road at the heart of the business district. All this information was available on their website. There were no pictures of the management on the site. Carl was not surprised.

The early part of Silom Road is where you can find Patpong Road. Patpong was the more famous red light district and was born in the latter part of the Vietnam War. Carl wondered how he had never crossed paths with this man, but in reality Carl had stopped being a permanent fixture at the bars of Patpong several years before Inman had arrived in Thailand. If Inman had been a regular visitor from Vietnam it would have been a few years prior to Carl's arrival in Thailand. Carl was pleased with the information he had gathered. It was enough for him to get started.

Surveillance in Thailand never worked the way it was depicted in foreign films and television programs. It was typically a series of failures: watchers not getting where they were supposed to be at the correct time, losing the target in traffic, and not being able to enter the same places as the target due to their speech and dress reflecting their lowly place in Thai society. It was also relatively expensive. Surveillance was the only service that Carl had provided that led to demands of fees being refunded. Something Carl was loath to do, and rarely did.

Carl sometimes used a team of plainclothes detectives from his local police station that would do a reasonable job of following someone, but they were expensive and clumsy, often putting them at risk of being spotted. So Carl opted for loose surveillance provided by a man he knew who had his own taxi. With the help of his son, he could tail almost anybody. The taxi was never noticed among all the other taxis on Bangkok's streets and the son was there to jump out and follow on foot when necessary.

Carl telephoned his man and told him he had a printed picture, a home address from the ID card record and an office address and when could he start? Boonchoo said he could start immediately. He always said he could start immediately. Carl paid well and he liked people who appreciated it; not many do.

Next Carl called the colonel. Colonel Pornchai always behaved towards Carl as if he was doing him a favour as opposed to doing business. The colonel dragged his feet and complained about every requirement and Carl pretended he didn't know he was paying double what he should. That was how the game was played and the men in uniform always had it their way, or they simply changed the rules. Carl understood the rules and had learnt to play the game well.

He didn't mind paying more money to the colonel instead of contacting his less expensive immigration contact directly. It brought the colonel into the game and that gave Carl access to a larger network that could be called on for protection if needed. They were not the types to let anything happen to somebody foolish and naïve enough to pay them double market price. They agreed on the inflated budget to check the immigration computer twice daily despite the colonel's protestations of how difficult it was under the military government. Carl would be informed almost immediately the next time Somchai Poochokdee boarded a plane to Hong Kong or Macau.

Carl enlarged the target's picture from the ID card record printout and hand wrote the relevant details, which he put in a brown envelope and took downstairs and gave to his maid telling her it was to be collected by Khun Boonchoo or his teenage son.

His maid was a hag and he allowed as little contact with her as possible. She had come with the rented house and as much as he wanted to get rid of her he assumed she had nowhere else to go. She had worked there for at least twenty years and was expecting to be there after Carl moved on. She took his tolerance as weakness and had become even more impossible to deal with. The thought of her sleeping under a bridge had started to appeal to him.

"You no nice to Thai lady. You no have wife you, because you no smile. You too old wait. Must marry. Thai lady very nice but only like man who smile."

Although he was fluent in Thai she always spoke to him in her incoherent broken English. She was feigning concern for his lack of female company so she could act superior and remind him that all Thai people are better than foreigners. Carl did smile sometimes, just never when she was around.

He went back upstairs and spent the rest of Tuesday night lying on the sofa watching television. He fell peacefully asleep before midnight. He never remembered having bad dreams and had never been scared of the dark. A famous old Thai fortune-teller had claimed it was because the spirits enjoyed watching his antics and found him amusing, so they left him alone. Mind you, she also said he would be rich and famous after he turned forty. Nobody can be expected to be right about everything.

CHAPTER 7

Carl woke up Wednesday morning with the television still pouring out mediocrity. He turned it off and went quietly downstairs to the ground floor trying to avoid his maid and get his morning espresso. The maid was waiting for him. She told him that the taxi driver had collected the documents and gave him another irritating lecture on why he should learn to smile and adopt a whole rice farming community by marrying one of its daughters. Carl was pleased to hear that the target was already under surveillance. He almost smiled.

He went up to the sitting room on the second floor and carried the coffee and the laptop computer outside where there was a table and a couple of chairs. Carl looked around the garden and pool and saw that it was empty as usual. He looked at the buildings towering over the oasis and wondered why nobody seemed to use it except for him and George. Thai people typically spend their entire day hiding from the sun. This is not an easy thing to do as the sun shines almost all of the time.

The online news was mostly about Thailand settling down to its version of normal life under a military government. There was one story that got Carl's attention, the grief of the mother of one of the murdered girls. She had lost her temper at police inactivity and struck out at an unsympathetic junior police detective and been arrested for assault. She had been let go hours later when wiser senior officers stepped in to appease the Thai language tabloids.

The old, not so quiet Americans had told Carl on his first visit to the bars of Patpong that if he was looking for sympathy in South-east Asia he could find it in the dictionary between 'shit' and 'syphilis'. They told him that he had a fat chance of finding it anywhere else. At least some things could be relied on never to change. The family members of the killer's young victims would be left permanently traumatised. There wouldn't be any counselling and not much chance of any justice. They weren't rich or important enough to justify any serious effort or expense.

Carl checked his email account and saw a confirmation mail from his Singapore bank telling him that twenty-thousand dollars had been transferred from a bank in Latvia on behalf of a company called Victory Holdings. Apart from that glorious news all that he found in the inbox was the usual annoying advertisements and a pleasant message from an ex-girlfriend in creative advertising telling him that Alcoholics Anonymous had saved her and how it could save him too. Claiming she was still entitled to an opinion was her creative version of stalking.

All he could think of to say to her was how he belonged to a group he had created himself and had aptly named Alcoholics Unanimous. The solitary rule of this group was that, should any member not feel like having a drink, it was the responsibility of all of the other members to call him up and talk him into it. He didn't write the email. He never responded to invitations from his past. Life is about moving forward, always forward. That was the theory anyway. He thought it commendable that she had given up drinking. He would have been more impressed if she had given up evangelism.

Carl went into the house to get his phone. It was his habit to leave it upstairs in his bedroom for a while every morning. He had always found it best not to attempt speech in any language until after his second cup of coffee of the day. There were no messages on the phone and he had already seen his emails. Carl called the client's mobile but there was no answer.

Carl took the computer into the air-conditioned office and performed a deeper Google search of old newspaper stories. There was a story that stated the police were questioning fellow students in order to locate the latest victim's ex-boyfriend, their prime suspect. They had not taken into consideration the fact that many students moonlighted as cocktail waitresses and massage girls to engage in prostitution as a way to finance a normal lifestyle.

Carl assumed that the police were aware that a lot of the students sold sex. He would have been shocked if they hadn't known. Most of the policemen he had met over the years had slept with enough of them. Unfortunately, if the choice was to have an unsolved murder versus making an admission of the existence of such a sex industry in Thailand, then the decision was preordained. Thailand was not in the habit of peeling back the shiny silk cloth that covered its underbelly and allowing a peek at the eczema underneath.

The next thing he did was type in Somchai Poochokdee. There were no pictures of him, which didn't surprise Carl. He found a few press releases describing expanding real estate markets and charitable donations. It was an annoyingly superficial portrait of a respectable businessman. One positive find was a business article that included his office address, which Carl had already, and his mobile phone number, which Carl didn't.

Carl immediately sent a message to the colonel asking for a billing record of the phone number. This would take a few days, as the police would have to send an official request in writing to the phone company before they would release the

91

information. He then sent him another message suggesting they meet at the club at midnight. He didn't suggest an earlier time as nobody went there early.

George had entered the house through the door on the ground floor, which was where the kitchen was and the maid and the espresso machine lived. The maid liked George so he always climbed the stairs to the second floor with an espresso in his hand. Carl noted that George's coffee had a perfect head of brown foam, unlike the ones Carl usually got. He sat down in the armchair beside Carl's desk in the small office and sipped his espresso. He pointed at an eight by ten picture on the bookshelf behind Carl's chair. The photograph was mounted in an expensive wooden frame. It was a professional shot of an attractive black woman standing in front of a grand piano singing into a microphone.

"How is that going?" George asked.

"Not so well. I call that picture Bye Bye Blackbird."

"You don't want her to hear you saying that," George told him.

"Therein lies the problem."

"You think it didn't work out because she was black?" George asked.

"No, not that. The reason it didn't work out was because she was American."

"So you are still against political correctness?"

"Of course I am, it is a con. Fake politeness is not flattering, it is patronising. If a black person walked in here now are we supposed to put a governor on our conversation? That, George, would make us racists by default."

"It's America, Carl. The way things are."

"I don't have to behave like that and I sure as hell don't have to agree with it."

"Bye Bye Blackbird is actually quite funny," George said with a smile.

"It would be even funnier if it didn't need to be analysed and dissected before we dared reach that opinion."

"Do you miss her?" George asked. Carl didn't answer.

Carl brought him up to speed on the case details and the recent developments. George gave him a rundown on what he knew about the CIA in Vietnam, which turned out to be a lot. He said that he had met some good ones. He called them 'America's Dream Team' due to their high educations and strong beliefs.

He also spoke of a different sort. Men who'd turned the American dream into a nightmare. George said, "They were the corrupt leading the corrupt. Zealots for an imperial Christian America, with the sole purpose of making them and companies back home lots of money."

George looked around at the old books, oil paintings, worn Persian rugs, and the loudspeakers the size of wardrobes and amplifier from the industrial revolution. He squinted his eyes appearing embarrassed, then looked at the woman in the picture and asked, "She always asked me why you surround yourself with old things, I always wondered about your addiction to nostalgia too."

Carl pondered for a while and then said, "My theory, for your ears only, is that when a man doesn't know who he is then he goes back to the time when he thinks he did."

"Looking around this room, that would make you over a hundred years old."

"I hope you are not listening to the maid's theory of reincarnation. She thinks I am a born again arsehole."

George smiled, finished his coffee, and left by the door from the sitting room to the swimming pool area. Carl spent the rest of the day listening to music and reading the history of Beirut. Recently he listened only to classical music as his passion for jazz was not working any more.

A few kilometres from where Carl lived, Anthony Inman alias James Peabody alias Somchai Poochokdee was not having a good day. He was watching his prey taking her final tortured breaths but he had not enjoyed the process. This was the first time he was not excited by the metallic smell of bloody death or the faeces and urine smell of terror. The bitch had been too courageous and he had not felt the total control over her that would have been the climax of his art.

The little slut had still been spitting blood at him up until a few minutes before she had collapsed. She would die without total capitulation and that had made him very angry. "Fucking little cunt," he shouted at her loudly but she could no longer hear him.

She had called him pathetic so he had stuck a stiletto blade in her soft belly and she had screamed even louder. Somehow, between the screams, she had told him he was a limp-dicked sexual inadequate. All in perfect English too. So he had cut off one of the cunt's tits and she had spat blood on him, like a wild animal. She must have bitten off part of her tongue from the agony.

Then he had lost his temper. That was wrong. He'd never lost his temper before. He had gone a little crazy and stabbed her several times with the stiletto. That was why she was dying too quickly and he had wasted hours on her for nothing. "Fuck that," he said aloud again. Nobody was there to hear him and she had died, she was quiet now. He looked down at her with disgust. "Useless fucking cunt."

He left her on the floor and went to the bathroom to take a shower. He was covered in blood, her blood, that cunt's blood. He would leave her there and go home. He could come back the next day and clean up. Nobody would find her in the meantime. This was his safe place.

He hated her so much that he couldn't stand the thought of being in the same car with her. Never mind, he told himself. Tomorrow he would be better able to deal with it.

He put on some clean clothes and combed his hair with

pomade to smooth it and allow a neat side parting. He would go home to tell his wife and daughter that it had been a very bad day. He would tell them how an awful tramp with a tattoo and without the good manners to wear a bra or dress decently had said offensive things to him, and how he had nearly lost his temper.

They would look after him and make sympathetic noises. He would get a foot massage and a glass of aged tequila. They had always looked after him well and he felt blessed to have them. Perhaps he would use it as leverage to get a family Scrabble game going. Anthony Inman alias James Peabody alias Somchai Poochokdee liked playing Scrabble with his family.

Carl arrived at the club just after midnight. The club was a large elevated tubular building with somewhere in the region of a thousand people crushed together inside and queues outside. He had got the colonel the job running the security and put him in charge of keeping the authorities at bay with various financial incentive plans. Carl walked up the steps and was greeted by the bouncers who passed him through the red-roped area, much to the disgust of the long queue of hopeful patrons. He smiled at the girls on the reception desk as he walked past them and they put their hands together and raised them to their faces in the customary wai of respectful greeting.

Carl entered the modern music and light show by a sliding door that was supposed to protect the neighbouring buildings from the club's noise, but it spent as much time open as it did closed. Fortunately the first section of the bar nearest the door was reserved for the colonel as usual, so Carl didn't have to fight through the crowd. A bottle of Johnny Walker Black Label, a bucket of ice, and bottles of soda were already waiting on the section of the bar nearest to the door. He didn't wait for one of the pretty staff to come over but poured a drink from the bottle and waited for the colonel. The colonel was always fashionably late.

Carl looked around at the all-white room. The first time Carl had met the management was prior to their grand opening to discuss the need for a marriage between security and the local police. He had asked them why everything was all white and had been told in all seriousness that the nightclub was the canvas and the guests were the subject matter. Carl thought it was the last place on earth he wanted to be; there were no shadows anywhere.

The customers were models, trendy tourists, chic secretaries and the children of the rich. Some of the girls were semi-nude in their choice of high fashion and looked wonderful. For this reason Carl found it hard to dislike the place in spite of his incompatibility and the fact that it made him feel old.

The colonel eventually arrived with several young women following behind him and they all took up position at the bar. Viyada was the colonel's long-time girlfriend and chief accountant so she outranked the others and always took charge of pouring everybody's drinks.

Carl and the colonel had known each other almost twenty years. They had been involved in some serious situations and complicated cases together over the years. They had once had a gang of Nigerian conmen after them. The gang wanted their heads and not their wallets. After a dangerous battle of wits the gang was prosecuted and put in prison and the streets had become theirs again. The relationship was that of two people who had fought a few wars together. They didn't make a big fuss about money in their dealings but it was a business and money was the oil in their relationship, so Carl gave him an envelope with thirty-thousand baht in it and said, "Tell me when you need more."

"Thanks," he said. "I already paid immigration and I gave some to the captain for retrieving the phone record. What's this case?"

"A seventy year old runaway. Missing person. Client is the elder brother."

"As long as they pay the bills," he said laughing.

Various people came up to them and they spent the next couple of hours as regular people out for a drink on a work night. Gossip and voyeurism is not the worst way to spend the a.m.

A Russian model with her eye on access to

some power and possibly a fast-tracked visa extension turned her charm on Carl. She was beautiful and spoke a little English with a strong Russian accent. She was Hollywood fluff, a Bond girl inclusive of the long legs, tits, and rounded arse. She even came with a sensual enemy accent. A private detective's dream girl but unfortunately she was probably sixteen years old.

Carl knew the agencies in Russia would send young girls to Thailand as models and provide them with altered dates of birth claiming them to be much older than they actually were. The young models were much easier to sell so it was common practice. Carl politely made it clear that he wasn't interested. She went off in search of another person who could protect her. She was far too young and rare to be out so late on her own.

It was one of those moments when Carl cursed his seriousness and career choices. The ancient Greeks had been right when they said that knowledge could make you miserable. Better a little misery than the self-disgust that comes from behaving in a manner that stops you from being able to look at yourself in the mirror in the morning. That's what Carl frequently told himself and it seemed to help.

He still watched her naked back as she walked away though. He could just see the start of her muscular buttocks where the sunken back of her dress bounced as she walked. The colonel shook his head in disbelief at what he saw as Carl's old-fashioned foolishness. The colonel hated seeing a missed opportunity.

By two o'clock everybody was suitably drunk and the colonel and Carl moved off to one side.

"I need something and you won't like it," Carl told him.

"Not the first time. What is it?" He said smiling.

"I need case details on the student murders. I think the police are way off on their investigation. It is probably a foreigner and I may be able to point them in the right direction."

"They won't give that out. You are talking crazy." He was not happy but Carl had known that he wouldn't be.

"It is being handled by Crime Suppression. You have friends there. Just invite them here for a drink and bring it up in conversation after you have plied them with enough to make them drunk. The police are famous for being indiscreet when they're drunk so they'll tell you everything."

"We have an agreement not to interfere in active police investigations. Have you forgotten? Where's the profit in this?"

"I know, but I really need to know what is going on," Carl said casually.

"You must be drunk to be talking such stupid things," he exclaimed. "We should talk about it tomorrow."

"OK. Tomorrow when we are sober."

The problem was solved. By the following day the colonel would do what Carl had asked. When he was sober he would not admit that there was anything he couldn't do. He always came through for Carl but made a point of letting him know how much trouble it would cause him. He couldn't help it; he always went for the leverage. Leverage gets paid more. Carl claimed drunkenness and took his leave of the colonel and his harem.

CHAPTER 8

Carl drove the car a hundred meters and turned left. There was no point in letting the colonel know that he was happier drinking alone in the club around the corner. In Thailand people hunted in packs and Carl's lone wolf moments were beyond their comprehension. It didn't matter that they didn't understand him. He had ceased needing their approval long ago. Carl never followed the crowd for fear of getting lost in it.

If the colonel had known where he was going and that he would rather go there on his own he would have felt a loss of face, which is something that is taken very seriously in Thailand. Face was a big part of being Thai but remained an enigma to foreigners.

Carl had once been asked to explain 'Thainess', which had become the fashionable word to explain everything that was unexplainable to expatriates and tourists. He answered that the foundation of 'Thainess' was a desperate ambition to make it from birth to cremation without encountering serious embarrassment. He knew it was an oversimplification and therefore he was doing the Thai people an injustice but the audience had loved it. Carl played to his audiences and knew that they liked the shorter answers.

When the parking boys around the corner saw his Porsche they started shoving cars around until there was a big enough space for him to park. They usually required people to leave their car keys but Carl never did. He handed them a red hundred baht note and went to the back of the building. There were queues of people at the front door and an entry fee so he went through the back door. Carl used a lot of back doors.

Bar on Eleven was very busy and the customers were wall to wall. The club was constructed of smooth grey concrete. The walls were thick to keep in the noise, which made the outside of the building resemble a Second World War pillbox. The ground floor had a DJ and the music to match. The second floor was more laid back. It was not Carl's kind of music but the downstairs was a mix of actresses, models and high-class prostitutes so he sometimes put up with the noise.

He found a space at the bar that was big enough to stand in as long as he kept his elbows tucked in. Carl made a cramped hand signal for a drink and looked around the bar. The usual crowd was there, plus some ordinary people playing at being movie stars. Men with dyed hair and Botox faces wearing skin-tight Versace shirts and looking for the best love that money can buy. The women had spent the whole afternoon and early evening preparing their appearance in the hope that they might get noticed and win the lottery of life and get somebody to buy them a house. If it was all so wonderful why did so many of them end up so miserable? Carl knew that they weren't all as happy as they pretended to be. Some of them had been his clients.

The girls were dressed to kill. These were women and not the young girls you saw on Patpong, Nana and Soi Cowboy. They were hand polished, wore skimpy designer clothing, mostly bilingual and well travelled. Carl called them the Bangkok Hurricanes because they arrived with a lot of sucking and blowing and when they left they took your house. Most of the Bangkok Hurricanes didn't like him very much. Carl had been around way too long for their liking. Even the ones who didn't know him stayed away. Something in his attitude and body language told them he didn't own a house.

Eddie the DJ moved in beside him. He looked middle-aged Californian, probably because that was what he was. His hair was dyed blonde and he wore wire-rimmed glasses on a tanned face smoothed with designer creams and massages. There was an aura of naive optimism about him and his face looked younger than his body. Californians had something different, a perpetual youth that was typically spiritual rather than physical. Possibly something to do with the air in California or maybe the copious amounts of marijuana they had smoked at school.

Carl had got him out of jail once and Eddie had been eternally grateful. He had failed a urine test and his future had looked bleak. Eddie was scheduled to appear in court and advised to plead guilty to using drugs. Police would not be seen to involve themselves in assisting in drug related cases for fear they would be suspected of involvement in the trade. There was a war on drugs and it was not wise to be on the wrong side of it so the senior police were not available. Carl also didn't ordinarily touch drug cases but he had a soft spot for Eddie.

Carl had been made aware of Eddie's predicament the day after his arrest and he had done the only thing that he could think of. He paid thirty-thousand baht to a police private to drop a tray of urine-filled glass beakers on the stone floor of the police station. This was performed with much overacting and an almighty crash. Without evidence the case against Eddie and five strangers had been dismissed.

Somewhere in Bangkok five people who had never heard of Carl Engel woke up every morning and thanked police clumsiness for not having a criminal record. Eddie knew it was art.

"Hi Carl, good to see you," he shouted.

"How're you doing Eddie?"

"Same old, same old. If you need some coke it's on me. Just let me know, man. Anything you want," he said in a shout that was only a tone down from the last shout. It was lack of discretion that had got him arrested the last time.

"I'll pass on the Colombian marching powder. I need my sleep."

"Yeah sure. Hey what do you know about this serial killer? Fuckin' scary shit man."

"Not much Eddie. Why do you ask?"

"I've never had it so good man. If they catch him I'm seriously fucked," Eddie said in his low shout.

Carl studied him for a while and asked, "What do you mean, you're seriously fucked?"

"Hey man, everybody's scared and none of the girls in here want to leave with a stranger. They all know me in here. I've never had so much pussy in my life, man. There's a queue of them just hoping for a chance to buy me a drink or slip me a free E."

Carl laughed. "Never thought about it that way."

"Surprised the hell out of me as well, I don't want it to end. That's for damn sure. Don't get me wrong Carl. I still hope they catch him. You know what I mean, right?"

"Sure Eddie, I know what you mean. If you're

trying to make them all happy be careful mixing coke and Viagra. Remember what happened to Gianni?"

"Yeah, I remember. Fuckin' Gianni man. He was only thirty-three."

He had been following the progress of the music as he talked to Carl and he made a quick dash across the packed dance floor to the DJ booth. He always made it back to the turntables just in time to avoid an embarrassing silence.

Carl picked up his drink and started to look around the place. She had spotted Carl before he had noticed her standing in a raised corner with a group of the beautiful people. She was already looking at Carl when he saw her across the heads of the crowd. Her name was June and she was a marketing executive at one of the five-star hotels, which meant that she spent most of her working day in Starbucks drinking coffee and talking to her friends. Like a lot of beautiful women she was extremely insecure although you wouldn't know it to look at her.

Carl knew her without her clothes on and people say things when they are naked and it is three o'clock in the morning. It is not unusual for women in Thailand to have experienced some kind of sexual abuse whilst growing up. There are claims that as many as half of the women in Thailand have been raped or physically abused. It is a society built on levels of power and bullying is all part of the norm. June had her unfair share of dark secrets. The dynamic of abuse is the victim's need to cover it up. June lived behind a mask but Carl had seen what was underneath.

He was very fond of her but he knew a lot of that was because she made him feel like a hero due to her emotional dependence. He made damaged women feel safe, June had once claimed. She had told him he made her able to sleep without having bad dreams for the first time in her life. She always said such things when she was lying down and looking up at him with her big brown eyes. The relationship was made in heaven as long as they were lying down. When she stood up it was a whole different story and she was a very different person. It always ended badly, but such relationships typically do.

She separated from the group and pushed her way through the crowd. She was all perfect white teeth and waving arms as she got close to him. The people standing near to him moved away to avoid getting hit by her flying hands. June threw her bangle-adorned arms around Carl's neck and kissed him on both cheeks. The dress she was wearing was loose and shiny with a very low back that showed the top of her bottom. Maybe there was a sale on, thought Carl, remembering the dress the young Russian girl had been wearing in the club. When June leaned forward to kiss him he could see all the way down to her little G-string and bare buttocks.

"Carl, you bastard, where've you been? I was worried the gangsters had got you," she said in perfect English.

"Not gangsters, it was the police that got me," he replied over the noise.

"They are worse! You're joking, right?"

"Yes, only joking. They haven't got me yet."

"You should be careful. You make me worry all the time," she said with a frown that gave her dimples.

"How are you?" Carl asked her.

"Mad as hell you horrible person. Where have you been for the last year? I've been so lonely." She followed this up with a punch to his chest.

"I heard you had some old Hungarian man buying you diamonds and flying you first class to Paris and London for long weekends."

"What do you expect me to do? You'll never marry me," she said pouting.

"That is the story of my life June, I like to have rich friends but I can't really afford them."

She had got closer to him as the conversation progressed so Carl could hear her above the music. He could feel her warm breath in his ear and her breasts pushed up against him.

"Let's get out of here," she whispered, breathing right into his ear.

She said goodbye to her friends while Carl paid his bill. Somehow, her Champagne cocktails had been added to his bill even though she had not been standing anywhere near him when she had been sipping them. Carl had always wondered how they managed to do that with such efficiency in a country where it takes a week to change a light bulb. They left by the back door even though it wasn't really necessary. Carl took her that way because it always made her happy to show people that he was different.

They were in the car driving towards Carl's place. The roads were empty and Bangkok was a good place to be in the early hours of the morning. If you can be home by four in the morning and never go out until ten at night then Bangkok is probably an ideal place to live. The empty roads and the cooler night air made the Porsche a pleasure to drive. The air-cooled engine purred and roared along Sukhumvit Road. All the girls loved the passenger seat of the red Porsche.

June had taken her shoes off and had her feet tucked under her. Her head was resting on his left arm and bouncing every time he changed gear. Carl could see down the front of her dress and it looked very good. It was nice, comfortable and warm. They had been very good together once, for a while.

"Why can't we be together?" she asked him.

"What about your Hungarian?" Carl asked back.

"He's not important. He's in the business of

money, financial markets, something like that. You know the type. My friends call him Sashimi, cold fish. I am lonely and bored Carl, all those money guys are the same, no warmth, too serious and always working. I am happy when I'm with you. I like how you make me feel. I never get bored when we're together."

"We tried it June, remember? It is all happy and wonderful until one day you can't have a two-hundred-thousand-baht handbag or a first class ticket to Europe. Then the trouble starts."

"I don't want anybody else. I don't care how rich they are," she said, meaning it, or meaning it at the time she said it to be more precise.

"June, this is me and this is my life. I'm not making a career change at my age and I'm not apologising for not being born with a silver fork in my tongue. You always love me when another man is paying your bills. Last time we moved in together it was a catastrophe. You may be happy to be with me but we both know you will never stop flirting with other men's bank accounts," Carl told her sternly.

"You make me sound like a whore." Her face was becoming red with anger and she was sitting rigidly straight.

"I am just saying this is the way it is."

"Fuck you! Stop the car!"

A fuck was already out of the question so he gave her half of what she had asked for and stopped the car. She grabbed her shoes and designer handbag and leapt out of the car in bare feet slamming the door behind her. Carl lit a cigarette as he watched her beautiful rear disappearing angrily into the distance. He hated to see her go and there had been a time when it took him a while to get over her. Carl felt regret that she was gone again. What bothered him most was that under all of the conflicting emotions he mostly felt relieved. He had once been accused of having an overly protective subconscious that looked after him without him being aware of it. Maybe they were right and, who knows, maybe he had pissed her off on purpose. "Carl," he muttered to himself as he drove home, "can you really afford to be throwing beautiful women out of your car in the middle of the night?"

CHAPTER 9

Carl located his client late Thursday morning. The fat man was beside the hotel pool and he was not alone. His companion was obviously a bar girl but he appeared convinced that nobody else in the hotel was aware of that. Carl didn't recognise her so he assumed she came from Nana Plaza on Sukhumvit Soi 4. He hardly ever went there. He had never liked it much and found the bars there more aggressive than the ones in Soi Cowboy. There was only one way in and out of Nana Plaza's bar complex and Carl didn't approve of that either. Carl liked lots of options when it came to making a fast exit.

The client had the demeanour of a man who was happily living a celebrity lifestyle with a young model attached. What the rest of the world saw was an elderly, grossly overweight sweating foreigner, holding hands with a micro-bikini clad teenage girl with plastic tits, fuck me tattoos, bright green fingernails and a permanent scowl. The client had an expression on his face like he had won the lottery of life. 'It must be so much more fun to be oblivious to public opinion,' Carl thought.

Carl had a quick look around the pool area. It was laid out like a tropical garden with palm trees and dark wood salas, providing some shade. The sala is the Thai version of the gazebo. The largest sala was used as the hotel's poolside restaurant with cushions on the floor for sitting cross-legged at low oblong teak tables. This was where the pool staff congregated.

Carl spotted a sweating muscle-bound security officer in a dark suit hiding behind the cashier's booth at the back of the poolside restaurant with his two-way radio in his right hand. He was staring at their table and talking excitedly into the radio. Carl was friendly with the security team and hoped they wouldn't hold today against him.

Five-star hotels preferred Bangkok's working girls to stay away from their swimming pools. Most of them had a policy of allowing the girls into the hotel as long as they let security take a photocopy of their ID card. This was in case a guest later claimed he had been robbed. This semi-open policy was necessary to keep their guests happy. This was Bangkok and not everybody came for the temple tours and the fake handbags.

The hotels believed this policy worked in a discreet enough fashion that the other guests would never know what was going on.

Unfortunately for the hotel, they had a guest staying with them who was not familiar with the rules and was advertising their secret compromise to the other guests.

There was not a lot the hotel could do about her. They would have had her registered as staying in his room for their legal protection. So for all intents and purposes she was their guest. They wouldn't have minded so much if she had been even half presentable. Unfortunately for the hotel she had almost everything they disapproved of. If the word 'Prostitute' had been tattooed on her forehead she would have been holding a full house. Carl's client was oblivious to the drama being played out in front of him.

They sat down at a poolside table. Carl sat in the chair opposite the client, which put the girl with the green fingernails on his left. She was devouring plates of spicy food as if she hadn't eaten for a week. The next few minutes involved the usual circus of having to say something to her in Thai because the client insisted that she would be impressed. She wasn't, but Carl humoured him anyway.

"So, to be honest, I wasn't expecting to hear from you so soon. What have you got for me?" he demanded in a tone that assumed failure and wanted Carl to know that he was expecting nothing but excuses. He was sweating profusely and his pasty white skin was quickly turning bright red in the sun. This was good news for hotel security. Carl wondered if they realised it.

Carl heard a beep from his phone telling him that a message had been received. He took his phone out and held it under the table away from the glare of the sun. He took his reading glasses from his pocket and perched them on the end of his nose. The message was from the hotel's head of security. It said, 'please call me when you get a chance.'

"Please excuse me for a moment. I need to answer this," Carl told his client.

He typed in a reply that said, 'I know what you want. Don't know him well enough to criticise his taste in women. My guess is sunburn will get you the result you are hoping for.'

Carl put the phone away and carefully placed a blown-up picture sourced from Somchai Poochokdee's Thai ID record on the table. Then beside it he put documents regarding structure and ownership of Las Vegas Real Estate. He turned the documents around so they faced the client. Then he added some digital printouts of pictures of the target's office, home and car.

"The name he is using is Somchai Poochokdee. He took on this name when he became a Thai citizen in 1997. He got his Thai citizenship much faster than I have ever seen done by anybody before. He owns and operates a company called Las Vegas Real Estate. The office was on Phetchburi Road but was moved to Silom Road several years ago. I have a surveillance team mobilised and on him since yesterday. He lives in a large house in the suburbs of North Bangkok and is married with a teenage daughter. His wife is still a bit of a mystery but the team say she looks well educated and from a good family. They put her age at early forties. I am waiting on her family history. His travel records show frequent visits to Macau where he plays poker and my information is that he has been doing this for over a decade. He travels on a Thai passport."

The client lifted the picture to within a few inches of his face and creased up the skin around his fat eyes to squint the picture into focus. He placed the sweat-drenched paper back on the table and became temporarily speechless. When he did attempt to speak it was mumbled and incoherent. He took a deep breath and said, "It's him. That's my brother. How did you do it?"

"I have my methods," Carl answered trying to sound humble. Well, maybe he didn't try that hard.

"What now?" the client asked.

Carl appeared to think for a while. In reality his pitch had been planned in the car on the drive over. For reasons he didn't understand at the time, he had chosen not to mention that he was doing a background check in the USA.

"Surveillance to understand how he functions, telephone records to see who he talks to, general information sourcing to try to link him to the victims. I'm networking into the police investigation of the student murders. I cannot begin to tell you how dangerous it is to be seen to be interested in such an active high profile murder case. I'm trusting you will maintain secrecy until I have completed the investigation," Carl told him in his professional voice.

"Good. Of course, I understand. To be totally honest I am too excited to think and will happily follow your advice. I'll wait to hear from you again."

Victor, the fat man, was dismissing him. It was a quick end to the meeting, which was very unusual under the circumstances, even with the danger of sunburn looming. Carl was usually able to anticipate how his clients would react to information and would structure his strategy accordingly. This was not something he had planned for.

"One more thing," Carl said not getting up from the table. "Next time he goes to Macau I want to fly there and sit down at the game. I want to sit across from him without him knowing who I am. I want to look into his eyes and see what's in there."

"What will you need?"

"An additional ten-thousand dollars should cover it."

"It'll be sent in the next half hour," he said as he signalled the waiter for his bill.

Carl found the whole meeting curious, very curious indeed. The client's agreement to his request came too easily for Carl's liking. Alarm bells were going off in his head but he ignored them. He was going to Macau to play in a big poker game with a suspected serial killer. It sounded like too much fun for him to worry about a little thing like alarm bells in his head. The first lesson in surviving on the streets is how important it is to trust your instincts.

Carl said goodbye to the client and his semi-detached companion, got up from the table and walked past the poolside restaurant on his way to the swimming pool exit and the lifts. He winked at the security man as he walked past. The man smiled in embarrassment and reported Carl's departure on his radio.

He took the lift to the basement where there was an unmarked door that took him into the head of security's office. Jack Burke was at his desk in the windowless room studying the cryptic crossword in that morning's Bangkok Post.

"Morning Jack," Carl said as he took a seat.

Jack Burke looked up from his newspaper and smiled. "You've got strange friends Carl. It's one of the things we like about you. Never a dull moment when Carl is around, we tell each other at morning meetings. The only thing is Carl, why the fuck do they all have to stay at our hotel?"

Jack had taken the queen's shilling in his youth and served honourably for three decades. After retirement he had taken a long holiday in Thailand, where his straight back and military bearing had landed him the position as head of hotel security. Carl approved of him in spite of his habit of wearing short-sleeved white shirts and his regimental tie.

"You can't put this one on me," Carl told him, "he was already a guest here when I met him."

"Client?"

"Possibly, I think he's feeling me out. God knows I could do with one at the moment."

Jack looked up from his crossword. "Been playing with a cold deck again, have you?"

"Something like that. Can you ask your boys to keep an eye on who visits him at the hotel? It would be useful to know if any lawyers or other PIs are sniffing around."

"Sure Carl. They never mind doing you a favour."

"Please let them know that I always appreciate it," Carl said as he got up to leave.

"No problem," Jack said as he got back to wrestling the crossword. "This one's got me stymied; a meal fit for a prince or a rover? It's two words."

"We should get together at Paddy Murphy's for a pint one night when the football's on."

"Look forward to it. You're buying," Jack told him without looking up from his paper.

"Dog food," Carl told him as he went out the door.

The Porsche went quickly and noisily through the car park's twists and turns. Its rumbling deep bass engine set off car alarms as it went past them. The red monster shot down the hotel ramp and into Bangkok gridlock. Carl patiently drove through the heavy traffic to his destination on the river, ducking in and out of lanes with great skill as Bangkok drivers are expected to do.

He arrived at River City shopping centre over an hour later. His car didn't like daytime Bangkok traffic and its air-cooled engine suffered from the midday heat and lack of speed. The monster's roar had become a whine and like a horse ridden too hard it needed a few hours of stabling.

River City was the antique market specialising in expensive furniture and Buddha amulets. It was located on the Bangkok side of the Chaophya River and catered to tourists and wealthy locals. Carl parked the tired Porsche on the third floor and entered through a door marked Fire Exit. He walked past the shops with their high-priced antiques to a Thai seafood restaurant with a view across the water to the Thonburi side. The other side of the river had always been the less expensive half of the city, as it did not cater to many foreigners.

Carl sat at his regular table facing the river and ordered an iced tea and a plate of pad thai noodles with fresh prawns. The restaurant staff kept the table for him whenever possible.

There was an apartment building on the other side of the river that Carl could see best from that particular table. He had regularly watched it for several months but didn't do so every day. He couldn't see anything of importance anyway, as it was too far away for normal eyesight, and he didn't bring binoculars.

The building under surveillance was a relatively modern condominium with a swimming pool and terrace facing the river. Residents could access it by taking a boat from the pier next to River City, thereby never actually having to interact with the Thonburi half of Bangkok's vast metropolis.

Carl easily identified the balcony window belonging to apartment 5C because he had stayed there many times – that and the bright orange curtains. It didn't matter to him that he was too far away to see any people moving around inside. He already knew what the inside of the apartment looked like.

At that time of day, the woman in the photograph he kept on his bookshelf would be singing standards and exercising her vocal cords.

She would be in the white dressing gown he had stolen for her from the Oriental Hotel and she would be wearing nothing else. He imagined her lithe dark body under the white towelling. She was probably singing Misty. She usually sang Misty when she exercised her vocal cords.

He enjoyed having lunch at the seafood restaurant. It was never pre-planned that he drove there in the middle of the day through the lunchtime traffic. It just happened sometimes. It had been happening quite a lot lately.

CHAPTER 10

Early Friday morning Carl received the phone call he had been hoping for. It was from the colonel telling him that Somchai Poochokdee had boarded a plane to Macau late Thursday. Carl had packed an overnight bag in readiness and it was waiting for him on the middle of his desk with his passport. Carl knew the target's habit was to spend a couple of long weekends in Macau every month so it had not required deductive genius to know he would be rushing to the airport sooner rather than later. The magnetic pull of clinking chips and playing cards fluttering across green baize had made it difficult to sleep. Carl was exhibiting all the impatience of a child at Christmas.

Carl was excited that he was going to be able to meet his prey and get a good look at him up close and personal. The client's story had sounded credible enough up to a point but Carl found it overly convenient that Bangkok's serial killer had been handed to him on a plate. He had never had one before and had never expected to get one so easily. The case had finally got his full attention.

At the time Carl had not believed the claim that the long lost brother was also a serial killer. Clients have a tendency to vilify their chosen targets to private investigators and lawyers in the belief that it will get them better service. That and the comfort they got when they believed that they had recruited an accomplice as opposed to a service provider to help fight their cause. Carl had found the client's claims of having a serial killer in the family a little too topical for his liking. Private detectives and clients read the same newspapers in the morning. He had heard lots of stories in his time and rarely believed everything his clients told him.

He had spent the previous evening counting out money and studying his poker books so when the call came he would be ready for action. Carl had also searched the Internet and listed the phone numbers of the major casino hotels in Macau. He made a coffee from the espresso machine, took it upstairs, lit a cigar and got on the phone.

"Good morning can you put me through to Mr. Somchai Poochokdee's room please."

A pause and then, "We don't have a guest by that name."

"Thank you." He hung up.

On the fourth attempt he was waiting for a response at the end of the pause but instead got the sound of a phone ringing in one of the rooms. He hung up the phone immediately. The target was staying at the Venetian Hotel and Casino in Macau. Carl made an online airline booking to fly to Macau in the afternoon and booked himself a room at the Wynn Hotel and Casino. He was not going to stay at the Venetian Hotel, as it would have made it too easy for the target to get his real name.

Carl checked and confirmed that the ten-thousand dollars was in his Singapore bank account. The money was already there and he wondered if he was letting his suspicions get the better of what was so obviously good for business. He found it hard not to feel a certain fondness for a client that gave him large sums of money so quickly and easily. Carl felt that sometimes he had quite a lot in common with the girl with the green fingernails.

Carl was standing in his office and going through all of his standard last-minute actions before getting a taxi to the airport. He checked his passport to make sure his re-entry visa was properly dated and stamped. He printed out his ticket with all the required reference numbers. When he checked his emails, he saw that the background check he had asked for had been emailed to him by his contact in Los Angeles. There was also the daily report from Boonchoo. Carl printed both emails including attachments, put them in his bag, and left for the airport.

Once in the taxi Carl made the necessary phone calls. He rang George to tell him he was on his way to the airport and would be out of contact at least until Sunday. George told Carl he already knew what time the flight was. He had heard it from the compound's underground maids' network. Remember, it is only a secret until you tell somebody, Carl reminded himself.

The next thing Carl did was to call the colonel. He told him he was going to Hong Kong. If he had said Macau the colonel would have assumed that he would end up broke which would not be good for the colonel. Most people leave their money at the casinos, and the colonel's friends, like most Thais, were fearless gamblers, betting incredible amounts on the turn of a card at the baccarat tables of Macau's casinos. Fortunes were sometimes lost in a single weekend. So Carl created a story of a small job that he needed to do in Hong Kong to avoid a lecture on the evils of gambling. Before they ended the call the colonel told him he was meeting some police associates on Saturday night and would ask them what they knew about the student murders. The colonel said one of his friends was in the department that was investigating the most recent cases.

Carl felt he had everything under control. Thinking everything was under control was always a foolish thing to do. It was Asia and anything could happen.

The last call on his list was to the old man working the surveillance.

"How is it going?" Carl asked him.

"Nothing much happening. He goes to work and goes home. We took pictures of his car, his house and his office. I send you all the pictures daily by email. Last night he went to the airport with a bag. My son went to the noodle shop where his staff eat their lunch and heard that he is due back in the office Monday morning."

"Very good. Take the weekend off and start again Monday morning."

"Thank you," he said. Then before Carl could hang up he continued. "Just one thing. There was an unusual event at 2:35 yesterday afternoon. He had a very loud argument with another foreigner at his office. It started outside on the street when our subject arrived in his car. He was confronted and then the argument continued as they went upstairs shouting at each other. The foreigner doing most of the shouting left about fifteen minutes later. He was smiling when he left. My son jumped in another taxi and followed him to the Sukhumvit Grande Hotel."

"What did he look like?" Carl asked, dreading the answer.

"Very old and very fat. I have a picture."

"That's all right, I know who he is. We will talk again on Monday. Thank you."

Shit! Never trust a client. The case was flowing nicely and everything was in place and then his own client blew his cover. He hadn't considered the possibility, even though these things happened. They happened a lot. Carl should have been used to it. But, more importantly he should have planned for the possibility. It was extremely foolish of him to assume that on whatever case he was working on, that this time everything was going to be different. Clients were impatient and acted foolishly.

Carl needed to rethink his situation before he got to the airport. Anthony Inman knew that he had been found but had still gone to Macau. That could mean he was not concerned or it could mean that he was. So it made no difference to Carl's understanding of his new situation. Was there any reason to believe that he would be aware that it was Carl who had located him? Not likely, but certainly not impossible. Would he take it personally if he knew it was Carl? No reason to think so. Most people didn't. As long as he was not a raving lunatic he should see Carl as a nuisance, not an enemy. Like a person being sued would feel towards the lawyer retained to sue him. Not that Bangkok private investigators had the luxury of assumed respectability that often protected lawyers.

Reality check. All Carl really knew was that he didn't know very much. The real decision to be made was whether or not he should get on the plane to Macau. He found the adventure was irresistible so he had spent ten minutes doing mental gymnastics for nothing. Of course he was going to Macau.

Carl arrived at Suwarnabhumi Airport with plenty of time to kill. He strutted in like he owned the place to cover up the stress that had taken a grip on him in the taxi. Airports are not good places to be seen acting nervous and upset in. Not unless you liked being touched up by a gorilla in a uniform. He avoided the new automatic check-in machines and went to a counter with a human being behind it. Carl was old-fashioned about such things.

The name of the airport should be a warning to visitors. The unpronounceable name 'Suwarnabhumi' for an airport built to receive millions of visitors who don't speak Thai is a declaration that the locals are planning to have it all their own way. The correct pronunciation is soo-wah-nar-poom but only a handful of foreigners can work that out from the complex spelling. Typically when tourists asked Carl how they should pronounce it to Bangkok's taxi drivers so they could be understood, Carl always told them, "Airport!" That worked most of the time, he told them.

Carl spent the long journey from the security check to the departure gate trying to work out what had been bothering him since the first day when he had taken the case. The long distance walk gave him plenty of time to think. The conclusion he reached on arriving at the departure gate was that it was the money. The money had come too easily for Carl's subconscious to be comfortable with. The rest of Carl had of course been ecstatic. The voice at the back of Carl's head was reminding him of something. It was saying that people who pay that much money and that easily usually have a guilty conscience. Carl put his doubts aside for the second time. He was going to Macau and he was going to play poker with somebody else's money. What could possibly go wrong?

Once in the air he soon wished he had stayed on the ground. Carl had taken a Bangkok Post newspaper from the rack at the door of the plane. He waited until the plane had taken off before opening it. He had only taken it for the cryptic crossword. A quick glance at the headlines on his way to the cryptic crossword was his habit. Unfortunately Carl got stuck on page three and never made it to the crossword page.

He had noticed a small headline in the top right hand corner with a couple of paragraphs below it; a seventy-year old tourist had been shot outside the Sukhumvit Grande Hotel. Victor Boyle, a tourist, had been shot Thursday evening as he left his hotel. A motorcycle with two men in dark clothing and wearing black crash helmets had pulled up beside him as he was getting into a taxi.

They shot him three times and fled through the Bangkok traffic. The paper reported they were believed to be professional killers as the shooter had calmly walked up to his victim and checked for a pulse before fleeing. The deceased was said to be a very large man and a US citizen from the state of Nevada.

After all the years Carl had been operating as a private investigator it had finally happened; he had lost his first client. Who the hell was Victor Boyle? Carl thought his name was Victor Inman like his brother. He hadn't checked which was stupidity bordering on total incompetence.

He went to the luggage locker above his head and took the background check on Anthony Inman from his hand luggage. Carl sat down, put his glasses on, fastened his seatbelt and started reading. It was all there as he expected; the marriage and divorce, the children he had abandoned, and his company directorships. There was no mention of him and the CIA of course. It was pretty much what Carl had been told by his client. There was one glaringly obvious thing missing though; Anthony Inman didn't have a brother!

CHAPTER 11

Macau from the air was only recognisable to Carl from its shape and the location of the bridge that joined the two parts. It had gone from being a sparsely populated island to a neon metropolis. He had last been there in 1979 for a day. He had arrived on the hydrofoil from Hong Kong to seek his fortune at the tables. Carl left Macau that night for Hong Kong, on the last boat out, with empty pockets. The tables had not been kind.

The last time Carl had been a teenager. Now, over thirty years later, the memories were patchy. He remembered arriving back in Hong Kong and eating a cheeseburger from a fast food outlet. It was all he could afford and a novelty as the factory made semi-synthetic food hadn't invaded Thailand at that time. After that Carl went to the famous Bottoms Up bar and found himself unable to finish a whisky soda. This was something he found curious indeed. Carl returned to the very cheap hotel he was staying at and went straight to bed.

Carl woke up two days later. He was bright yellow and too weak to walk to the bathroom. He remembered rallying all his strength and crawling there to vomit continuously. He somehow found the strength to get back on the bed where he passed out and didn't come to until another twenty-four hours had passed. Whatever it was, it was very bad. Carl thought he was dying but hoped survival was not out of the question. Staying in the hotel room was not feasible. He was almost out of money and if he stayed any longer the bill would exceed his wallet. Carl decided to die in Thailand instead of Hong Kong.

He had an open return ticket to Bangkok so he called downstairs and asked them to book him a seat for that afternoon. Carl put on sunglasses to hide his yellow eyes, summoned strength from who knows where, and got a taxi to the airport. The only thing he could remember about the airport was dragging his bag across the airport floor because he had been too weak to lift it. The bag had only weighed eight kilos.

The next few weeks were a blur but even in his confused state Carl immediately made a decision to avoid all alcohol and unhealthy food for a year. He moved into a wooden shack surrounded by Bangkok's poor due to lack of funds and his inability to work. It was not a bad year as he soon got a grasp of slum politics. Carl's liver recovered and his Thai became fluent. He walked out of the slum community into a new decade. The year was 1980.

He had been totally penniless but that was not a problem. The first task was to survive, always survival first. He came out of his wooden shack fluent in Thai and having developed a better understanding of the intricacies of unseen Thailand. Carl returned to his old haunts, but this time he had something foreigners needed and were willing to pay for.

Carl landed at Macau airport remembering how disastrous his last visit had turned out and hoping better luck would be waiting for him. Maybe the gods of gambling would pat him on the head and say, 'Good boy Carl, it's your turn today.' Mere mortals create such dreams and think such thoughts.

He checked into his hotel, took a shower, and then went to the Venetian and took a walk through the poker room. The target was not there. Carl assumed that the best games started in the evening and went on through the night. They typically did. The target was probably sleeping all day and would be back to the tables later. Carl had a few hours to kill.

He left the Venetian and went for a walk in the old town to see if he could find anything familiar. He found the old square and church built by the Portuguese. Beyond that it was unrecognisable. A modern Mecca for Chinese gamblers and as almost every Chinese is a gambler, no expense had been spared to lure them through the doors. Carl went back to his room at the Wynn Casino to escape the madness. A period of meditation on the art of poker before the sun went down seemed like a very good idea.

That evening he took up position outside the poker room so he could see his target arrive. Carl didn't have to wait long. Inman walked quickly, in gavotte steps, his head switching left and right in perfect time as if his neck was wired to his feet. He was tough and wiry in the way that old soldiers are. His skin was dirty brown like old leather and he had the most piercing eyes Carl had ever seen. Like a hawk's eyes, an old hungry hawk.

The staff and the room manager treated Inman like he owned the place. For the first time Carl felt totally alien, a complete outsider and a long way from home. He thought about leaving, getting his bag and going to the airport. Nothing was stopping him. His client was dead and he had enough money to disappear for a while. Take a holiday and forget he had ever heard of these people. Without doubt the most sensible course of action. Carl had always understood other people's madness better than his own. If someone in a similar situation sought his advice Carl would have provided ten excellent reasons to walk away. Carl however, of course, walked into the poker room and proceeded to act like a tourist.

Carl had dressed for the part. Black soft leather Aldo Brue shoes without socks, black Gucci jeans, black Zegna shirt, and a black cashmere blazer from a tailor in Milan. He looked like a tourist planning a big night out on the town. A tourist with pockets full of money was exactly how he wanted to be perceived. The modern poker players typically wear nylon and spandex topped off with a baseball cap so it is not hard to make an impression in a poker room.

Carl went over to the board and looked at the various games that were available. Inman had been directed to the table that required a player to buy a minimum of HK$ 50,000 worth of chips before sitting down. Fortunately the table still had empty seats available.

Carl asked the room manager about the games and intentionally showed no interest in the low stakes seats that were available. When the room manager said there was a seat free at a larger stakes table Carl told him that would suit him just fine. The room manager had a sad-faced pockmarked boy take him to the table and seat him. 'The game's afoot,' Carl thought. He liked the words and as Conan Doyle had stolen them from Shakespeare Carl didn't mind stealing them from Doyle's creation, Sherlock Holmes.

"Good evening," Carl said to the six players at the table, expecting formality to cement his appearance as a tourist with money to throw away.

Five players ignored him but Inman answered.

"Welcome to the game. Is this your first time here?"

"Oh yes!" Carl told him. "I've always wanted to play live poker."

"Ah, so where do you play?"

Carl needed to set up the table if he was going to get an edge over them.

"Online. I play online. Sure, I know it's fixed, silly to play really. Does anybody actually win there?" Carl said in the fashion of the majority of disgruntled losers.

"You're right. It must be fixed. Here is much safer," Inman told him patronisingly. He bought Carl's whining act and looked pleased.

Cards were dealt and hands were won and lost. The other players were all Asian. There was a Japanese, a Thai and three Chinese who had their own conversation going and ignored everybody else. The Thai player was talking to Inman and it was obvious they knew each other well. Carl noted that Inman's Thai was pretty good, rigid and unnatural like most foreigners but his vocabulary was extensive.

They had both assumed that nobody at the table understood them so were openly discussing a land deal, Thai style. The Thai player's face looked familiar but Carl couldn't match the face to a name. He had a vague memory that he was somewhere on the fringe of politics, a deal maker and power broker. They were discussing how they could best steal 1,000 rai of land from the forestry department, bribe the land department to issue ownership documents, and then put it on the market for a small fortune. Inman started watching Carl with his peripheral vision and Carl realised that he was sensing that he was listening in.

He turned and stared Carl down with his hawk like eyes and asked him, "Have you ever been to Thailand?"

"I passed through a few times."

"Thought you might have," he said as he stared Carl down. He was very interested in him all of a sudden.

Inman and Carl were eyeing each other like two warriors across a battlefield that had lost all interest in the carnage separating them. Carl had hands, he raised and Inman folded. When he made a move Carl got out of his way.

An uneventful hour passed. Then Carl looked at his two cards and saw a pair of nines. Inman raised the bet to two-thousand and Carl called with the intention of getting out quick if the flop didn't bring another nine. The young Chinese man on Carl's left called so there were three players in the pot. The flop came 9-4-4 and Inman bet seven-thousand. Carl only called his bet to trap him and then the young Chinese man pushed all his chips into the middle of the table. Inman pondered his cards and then reluctantly folded. Carl called the bet immediately with his monster of a full house. The player to his left turned up a King and a 4, both diamonds. Carl's full house was only vulnerable to another 4 coming, which would give the Chinese player four of a kind. The turn card was a blank and the river card was also not a 4. Carl had increased his stack of chips to around HK$ 110,000.

"That was exciting," Carl said.

"You too lucky. Shit lucky," the young Chinese man said.

"The winners make jokes and the losers say shut up and deal," Inman chirped, happy that he had folded his cards.

Carl thought of leaving with his winnings but he was there for a reason and all he had done so far was get lucky.

"I am just a student of the game and as a mere student I often find the game bloody murder," Carl said to the table but looking at Inman. "Do you find the game to be bloody murder?"

Inman looked at Carl curiously but did not answer. He continued to watch Carl as the game continued. Another hour passed with several dramatic hands but none involving Carl who had decided to play very tight and hold on to his money.

Then he looked down and saw a 7-8 of clubs, not much of a hand but he was the big blind so last to act before the flop. Inman raised his usual amount of two-thousand and Carl was the only caller. The flop was spread in the centre of the green baize. It was a 5 of clubs, 6 of clubs, and a Jack of diamonds. Carl bet six-thousand and Inman raised the bet to twenty-thousand.

Carl had a monster draw. He assumed Inman had a hand like Ace-Jack, which ruled out the possibility of him having a larger flush draw than Carl. So, that meant that any 4, any 9, or any club should win it for Carl. The 4 or 9 of clubs would give him a straight flush but that seemed like overkill. There were probably fifteen cards in the remainder of the deck that would win Carl the pot. With two cards still to come that made him a sixty per cent favourite to win the hand. That, plus what was already in the pot made it a good bet, a good raise to be more precise. However, Carl still had HK$ 100,000 in front of him and did not want to lose it all on one hand. Carl, unlike Inman, had limited funds to play with, so he just called the bet.

The turn card was a 4 of hearts giving Carl the highest straight possible. He wanted all of his chips in the middle now! Carl decided to be patient and therefore he checked to Inman. Who, without hesitation, bet HK$ 36,000 and Carl happily pushed all of his chips out in front of him.

"All in," Carl said as calmly as possible.

Inman immediately called his bet making the total in the pot HK$ 217,000. The huge pot that Carl had already assumed was his already.

Carl showed his hand and Inman turned over a Jack-Jack giving him three Jacks. This was not what Carl had wanted to see. There was another card to come and if that card paired anything on the table Inman would make a full house. There were lots of hands that would have had Inman drawing dead but unfortunately this was not one of them.

There were nine cards that would win him the hand, not ten as the 4 of clubs would have made his full house but given Carl a straight flush. Carl would win four out of every five times in this position. The problem was Carl couldn't afford to lose and continue to play. If he got unlucky and lost a pot of HK$ 217,000 which is about one million Thai baht, he would have had to leave the game. The altitude was going to put Carl at a disadvantage if he tried to continue with scared money. The air was thin and he was already getting dizzy.

The dealer seemed to take forever to turn up the final card. He looked around the table to make sure everything was in order. It was the biggest pot of the night and he had to make sure he was not at risk of being berated by the loser. He pulled the top card and burnt it, which is what they call throwing it into the muck with the other discarded cards. A tradition going back to the wild west where cheats often used marked cards. By throwing away the top card the dealer negated the advantage of a player knowing what it was. He then swiped the second card, let it hover for a while and then flipped it face up on the table for all to see. It was the Queen of hearts, which was a safe card for Carl. He had won the pot.

Carl had his head down, arms outstretched, pulling the enormous pile of chips towards him. The table was quiet, unusually silent. Carl looked up and saw him. Inman's face was white, his lips had become thinner, and his eyes shocked Carl. He had read books that had described a person as having hatred in their eyes. Carl had seen anger before but not such absolute hatred, nothing like this. The ice-cold eyes were projecting total rage. They were the eyes of a devil.

"You got very lucky Carl," he snarled.

What a voice, like something from somewhere else. The voice didn't fit the situation. And, fuck. He knew Carl's real name.

"But that is the last bit of luck you will ever have," he continued.

Carl kept stacking his chips.

"You will need that money Carl. You will need it to run. Thailand is that way and you want to be going the other way." He jerked his bony finger up and pointed west. "Try to run very fast and very far away. Life, as you know it is over. Amateurs don't last long in my jungle." He stared across the baize card table waiting for a reaction. He didn't get one. Carl was patiently stacking chips.

"You are beginning to bore me now. I do hope you are leaving," he said to Carl in a fake upper class British accent.

Then his face returned to normal. He dismissed Carl with his eyes and was done with him. The other people at the table hadn't understood the depth or the meaning of what he had said. They must have put it down to a temper tantrum resulting from hitting a dream hand of three Jacks and still losing over HK$ 100,000. Which was sort of what had happened.

The game resumed. He ignored Carl completely. Carl finished putting his chips in plastic racks and carried them to the cashier's window. He glanced back at the table and caught Inman looking at a nasty-looking Chinese male sitting at the bar. He was wearing a safari suit, had short cropped hair, a very square build, and a general look of mid-rank officialdom. Immediately after Inman had looked at him, he had looked directly at Carl. Carl converted his chips to cash and left the casino.

He directed the taxi to take him back to the street where his hotel was. Carl got out a hundred meters before the hotel and walked on the opposite side of the road to a restaurant directly across from the entrance. He was nervous and the hairs on the back of his neck were dancing the tango. Carl didn't have long to wait. Within a few minutes a car pulled up outside the hotel and parked illegally. Two men in safari suits got out and walked into the hotel. They were cops. Carl knew what cops looked like.

He expected them to have taken up position inside the lobby waiting for him to walk in. They would be certain he would show up eventually as he had not checked out and his luggage was still in the room. Fortunately his passport was in his jacket jockeying for space with the stacks of cash he had spread between all of his pockets.

In such a situation Carl found it was always essential to establish what adversaries were expecting him to do and then do the total opposite. Carl could live without his luggage so he pulled up the collar of his jacket, left the restaurant and walked, face down, up the street away from the hotel. He would head straight to the sea terminal and pay cash for a ticket on the first boat to Hong Kong. The same boat he had left Macau on all those years before.

CHAPTER 12

Carl landed in Bangkok late Sunday morning on a Thai Airways flight from Hong Kong. After queuing for the standard visa formalities and an unchecked walk through customs green channel he took a limousine from the airport to the city. The car's radio was playing North East Thailand's version of country music. Limousine drivers, just like the taxis, played their music whether they had a passenger or not. The traffic was unusually light and the sun was shining. Carl felt good to be back in Bangkok.

Carl was contemplating spending the next couple of days by the pool when the phone rang. The screen said 'George' so he answered the phone immediately.

"You picked up a tail at the airport," he told Carl.

"What kind of tail?" Carl felt a cold wave go up his spine. This wasn't the first time he had been followed but Carl had a premonition that this time was different.

"Looks like police to me," George said clinically.

"What kind of police?"

"Like undercover types. Nasty undercover types! The type of policemen that would stick a knife in your back, then arrest you for carrying a concealed weapon. I've got a picture of them on my phone, I'll send it to you." He sounded concerned and that bothered Carl.

"Okay I will see if I can lose them." Carl hung up.

At the early part of the twenty-first century, anonymous plainclothes police units had been executing suspected drug dealers as government policy. Police spokesmen admitted the body count to have been in the thousands. The executions had stopped after a shocked world had reacted loudly. There was no doubt that some of the executioners had killed people for their own profit or advancement in the criminal underworld. Many of the executed had not died well as the hit squads had tortured them for information and access to their money prior to dispatching them. The killings had stopped, or at least there was no overt government assassination policy anymore, but Carl knew the execution squads must still have been there, keeping a low profile somewhere in the police force. Carl hoped that the group following him was not from that background.

The phone buzzed and vibrated telling Carl that a message was coming in. He opened the attachment and looked at the picture of two men standing behind him as he queued at the airport desk to book the limo. They both wore safari suits, the Asian thug's uniform. He didn't know them and one look told him that he didn't like them. Carl put the phone in his pocket and told the limousine driver that there was a change of plan and to take him to the Hyatt hotel instead of his home address. Carl promised the driver a nice tip for the extra distance.

The next half hour had Carl feeling stressed. The mind did strange things when fear was thrown into the equation. He wasn't scared of death as much as the majority of people in the world. His life experiences had provided a certain level of immunity. The problem was being stuck in the car. The adrenalin wouldn't kick in until he was on the move. Then Carl knew he would stop feeling like throwing up and do what was required. It wasn't like this was going to be his first dance.

Carl asked the limousine to stop about fifty yards short of the hotel. He tipped the driver, as promised, and got out of the car. Carl walked casually into the lane that led to the car park and entered by the side door of the hotel. Just inside the door he loitered at the dry cleaning counter as if he was there to do his laundry.

Carl observed the car arriving with the two

men inside. They would have been harder to lose if they had been on a motorcycle but the car was their only option for an airport job because bikes cannot enter the elevated expressway from the airport to the city. An airport job requires a car. Carl watched one of them jump out of the car and walk towards him while the car drove off to enter the underground car park.

Carl walked past the hotel's trendy noodle restaurant, turned left and sat at one of the small tables outside the bakery nearest to the front of the hotel. A few minutes later both men walked into the bakery area and took up positions at the furthest table from where Carl was sitting. It was time to go as Carl had achieved what he was hoping for and got them both away from their car. Carl walked fast, almost running, to the street level front entrance. Past security, out the front doors and then a few yards dash into the street. There was a metal barrier the length of the hotel between the pavement and the road. Carl jumped over it and ran out into the road looking for a taxi with its sign lit up. He spotted one, stopped it in the middle of the road, jumped in and told the driver to take him to Patpong. Then he was moving away from the hotel. Carl saw through the back window of the taxi that his pursuers were still standing on the pavement outside the hotel. They were too surprised to have followed him over the barrier. Maybe they had been slow coming out of the hotel and didn't see him. It didn't matter. Carl was gone. Now he would get time to think.

On arrival at Patpong Road Carl went straight to the Madrid bar. It was a small bar in a single shop house with a heavy wooden door. The theme was built around oil paintings of Spanish bullfights and dark mysterious nudes. The Madrid was the only bar he knew that hadn't changed since the 1970s and it was a quiet place to have a drink in the afternoon. He badly needed a drink. Carl had to go through the usual pleasantries with the staff, as he was well known there. After his drink arrived the staff left him alone. They knew the rules. If he had wanted to talk he would have sat at the bar. As usual Carl was sitting in a booth.

As soon as he had started on his drink George walked in and sat opposite him in the horseshoe booth.

"How the hell didn't I lose you?" Carl asked.

"You did. Nice move, I saw it but was in the wrong place to follow you," George told him. "I just figured that you would probably come here."

"Thank God you're on my side," Carl said seriously.

"Yup." He replied laughing and then Carl started to laugh too.

George ordered an orange juice and waited for the waitress to leave before he spoke again.

"Might be a good idea if you told me what's going on," he said.

Carl brought him up to date. George's eyebrows went up when Carl told him about the demise of Victor Boyle and what happened in Macau.

"I hope you know what you're doing," he said after a moment's silence.

"I have to nail the bastard!"

"What about right now? It would appear that you are homeless."

Carl thought for a minute and replied. "I will get a new SIM card for the phone. They can tell where my phone is by triangulating the towers it uses whenever it is switched on. I will call you on this phone later and give you a number, deduct 500 from the number I give you and that will be my new phone number. Actually, it is better for me to get a new phone; otherwise they can track down the new number from the IMEI code on the old phone. Then I will check into a short-time hotel, one of the older ones with the curtains that pull over the parking spaces in front of the rooms. Not that I'll be using a car but these places don't require the usual registration process so I won't have to show ID. Those two things first, I need time to think."

"Do you have your iPod?"

"Yes, why would you ask?"

"Because you think better when you listen to opera and you are going to have to be brilliant. I am hoping for your best plan ever."

151

"I need you to do something for me."

"Sure," he said as Carl had expected him to.

"I need you to handle the old man and his son. They are tailing the target and it would be better if I went on silent running for a few days. I will call him now and tell him to report to you. If that's okay?" He nodded. Carl continued. "Use your old phone to communicate with him but get a new phone and only use the new phone to communicate with my new number."

"Done. You know what Confucius said?"

"What was that?" Carl asked him.

George wrinkled his face and squinted his eyes, "Confucius he say; private detective without client is like prostitute in room without a customer – probably only there to make self-entertainment."

"Point taken. Do you need some money?"

"No, that's not a problem. You can settle up with me later."

"If there is a later."

George ignored Carl's last statement and got up and left the bar. Carl called the old man and told him he was going out of town again so George would handle things. Carl also told him to be extra careful, as the target knew he was being investigated. Then Carl paid his bill and left the bar to look for a mobile phone outlet on Silom Road.

An hour later he called George and gave him his new number, having first added 500. As soon as he finished the call he switched off his Blackberry.

Knowing nobody could call him gave Carl a peaceful feeling. It was like going back in time to when nobody ever knew where anybody was.

He spent the next hour walking around in circles and performing tricks to see if anybody was following him. Having convinced himself that there was nobody there Carl went looking for a taxi.

In such a situation he would never take one of the taxis that worked the area and was parked waiting for a fare. Carl had found too many people by showing taxi drivers a photograph with a promise of money if they had ever taken the person in the picture anywhere and could remember where it had been. Sometimes it would take Carl all day to find the right taxi but he usually found them in the end. So Carl walked to the traffic lights at the junction of Silom Road and Rama IV Road and jumped in the back of an empty taxi that was waiting for the lights to turn green.

Carl arrived at one of Bangkok's seediest short-time hotels in the late afternoon. The one-storey hotel was located in a backstreet off Sukhumvit Road. He walked into the first room with an open curtain and entered through the open door. Carl sat on the bed and waited. A few minutes later a man walked in, stopped at the foot of the bed and asked, "Do you want short time or all night?"

It begged the question what he could have possibly thought Carl was planning to get up to for the next couple of hours alone in the room of a sex hotel. Carl politely told him he would need the room all night. Carl paid for the room and tipped the man five-hundred baht. Carl needed to be taken seriously and money was the currency of respect. If someone came sniffing around, Carl wanted to hear about it immediately. The man left smiling with the master room key in one hand and the five-hundred baht note in the other.

Carl got up and locked the door. He took the iPod from his pocket and selected The Magic Flute to listen to. He lay back on the bed looking up at the mirrored ceiling above him. It was time for thinking and George was right; he was going to have to be good.

CHAPTER 13

Monday morning finally showed up. Carl had been awake most of the night waiting for its arrival. He was bored and hungry, very hungry. Carl had not left the room the previous evening and so he hadn't eaten anything and his stomach was burning. He needed breakfast and was angry with himself that he was holed up in a room without windows, scared of hitting the streets. Carl decided that he was going to get a good breakfast and whoever was looking for him had better hope they didn't find him, not when he was in that kind of mood. Hunger and boredom made him brave.

Showered, unshaved, and dressed in the same clothes, he went out. Carl saw the man he had tipped the day before and called him over. Carl told him that he was on the run from an obnoxious wife and didn't want to be found. He put another five-hundred baht note in the man's hand and told him that he wanted to keep the room and to please not let anyone else in there. The man promised to lock the door and suggested Carl look for him when he came back. There were no guest keys. Carl wondered if the man ever slept.

There was a bar on Patpong that Carl had heard opened early and served American breakfast. Not the hotel buffet kind of American breakfast but the real, cooked on a griddle, eggs over easy kind of breakfast. He had his issues with the USA but had to concede that they were way ahead of the rest of the world when it came to making his favourite cooked breakfast.

Carl had been told that the place was owned and run by an old Texan and his wife. He had heard that they spent six hours every morning cooking and entertaining customers. The old couple would leave the bar at noon at which time it turned into a rather old-fashioned hooker bar run by their young manager. Funny set-up but Bangkok is a funny old town.

When you are on the run your priorities change. Carl could hide in a room with no windows or he could have a really nice day out. Hopefully, his toughest decision would be whether to have a massage after breakfast or stay at the bar and play with the girls. Playing with the girls would have been a delicate operation as his pockets were still stuffed with money and it was best if that didn't become common knowledge.

Carl had never been there for breakfast before, so nobody should be looking for him. As nobody would know him he thought he could have some fun playing the tourist for a change. He had often observed that the tourists appeared to have more fun.

Carl got out of the taxi right in front of the door to reinforce that he was a tourist. He could smell the country sausage cooking on the griddle before he opened the door. The booths were all occupied so he went straight to the bar and sat down. He could eat at the bar, he could talk to people, and he could even flirt with the waitresses. Carl was slipping comfortably into his chosen role for the day.

"Carl! What the fuck are you doing here? Off reservation for you isn't it?"

Bart bloody Barrows! The old Patpong hound. Man of all seasons. Early riser. The last person Carl wanted to bump into that morning. Bart went everywhere and talked to everyone so in a few hours the place they were in and the rest of Patpong would be off limits to Carl.

"Good morning Bart how's the daughter situation?" Carl asked him, trying to sound friendly.

"Little slut came home in the afternoon. I took away her mobile phone. That should fix her," he told Carl as he unsuccessfully tried to manhandle the passing waitress. "Never seen you here before," Bart stated as he let go of the very upset waitress.

"I'm not a morning person, but I heard good things about the breakfast here so I decided to make the effort."

"Is it necessary for you to talk like a damn limey all the time?" He didn't need anything from Carl today so any attempt at politeness was off the table.

"Well, Bart, that's what I am."

"Thought you were South African!"

"No, Bart, from a little town called London."

"Just kiddin', I knew that. You come from the land of lousy teeth, warm beer, fish and chips, and Princess Died. Did I get the name right?" He guffawed at his perceived wit. "Went there once. Didn't like it."

"Don't know much about it. I left the place at sixteen and haven't been back much," Carl told him trying to manage the conversation so he wouldn't let Bart annoy him any more than was absolutely necessary.

"Can't have been that good then, could it boy?" He pronounced it 'bwoy'. Only Bart Barrows would call Carl 'bwoy' after he was past the fifty years old mark. Something to do with Carl's having arrived in Thailand so young seemed to allow certain old Bangkok hands to claim superiority by not acknowledging that Carl had grown up.

Carl managed to eat his breakfast without telling Bart Barrows what he really thought of him. The grey-haired owner was telling Bart that he was not allowed to play with the waitresses in the morning. He had to wait until after noon for that.

Carl took the opportunity to get away without Bart noticing. Carl paid his bill hurriedly and left.

Bart Barrows had cost Carl his anonymity so it was back to the pavements. One of the side effects of believing that people want to kill you is an immediate need to procreate. Carl was aware that he needed to get laid sooner rather than later. He would require somewhere to hide as well. The short-time hotel was not good for his soul.

It occurred to Carl that he might as well make a little noise around the Patpong area. Bart Barrows, gossipmonger extraordinaire, had made it necessary for Carl to start avoiding Patpong. So, while he was still there he might as well make his presence felt. As long as the people wishing him harm ended up looking for him in Patpong they wouldn't be looking for him where he was really going to be. He walked the full length of Patpong Road without finding an open bar. It was still very early in the morning.

In a building just around the corner on Suriwongse Road at the Wild Orchid Bar, a place that Carl typically avoided, there would be an old man holding court. The famous American was known to be there every morning surrounded by his adoring fans. It was a place Carl rarely went to because it was common knowledge that this man didn't like him and vice versa. He was one of Bangkok's famous old Asia hands and was found fascinating by the barflies for having been the CIA's man in Bangkok prior to his recent retirement. Since his retirement he had spent every bad-tempered morning at the Wild Orchid Bar drinking himself silly. Nobody knew what he did in the afternoons.

Carl walked in and sat at the bar. He ordered a Bloody Mary. It felt like Bloody Mary weather. He was sitting in his usual spot, as Carl had expected he would be. Arthur Sciacci, 'Art' to his friends and fans, was a small feisty man with a crew cut. He had boxed Golden Gloves in his youth and still had plenty of scar tissue on his face to prove it. He was Texan-Sicilian by birth and a Langley man by design.

Art was at the corner of the bar, sitting on a stool just to the right of the door, turned sideways so he had his back to the wall and could see every movement and everyone enter and leave. He was talking at all the people around him, providing his daily update on world politics, which meant he was giving his evangelical opinion on what America was really up to that week.

The bar's regulars saw him as their Yoda, but Carl had always heard the rattle of Darth Vader and the dark side of the force in his voice. Art had seen Carl come into the bar and was watching him from his vantage point. Carl got his drink and felt Art's eyes on him analysing his every move as he started drinking the Bloody Mary.

"I ran into one of your old friends from

Saigon the other day. We had a drink together," Carl told him. "Anthony Inman I think his name was."

"No, you didn't. Inman died years ago," Art replied, full of confidence.

"No?" Carl asked quizzically. The game was on.

"No!" he said as he got off the barstool. He was standing at the bar, bouncing from one foot to the other boxer style and leaning forward in Carl's direction. "I'll tell you what you are up to." He was playing to the audience now, feet still and waiting for all eyes to be on him before continuing. "Carl is playing amateur detective. Over the last twenty years Victor Boyle has refused to accept that Inman's dead and has hired every private detective in Asia to find him. None of them could find him and Carl is the last detective to get the job, bottom of the list. Even an old friend of mine who spent twenty years with the FBI before going private was given this case and didn't find him so what chance does Carl have?"

Carl didn't want to ruin his morning by telling him that Inman had an office at the other end of Silom Road and had probably driven past the Wild Orchid Bar hundreds of times. Carl was planning to let Art have his fun for a while longer.

"How're you getting on with your client?" he asked Carl with a grin.

"Fine."

"Funny that, I heard he was shot dead on Thursday evening in front of his hotel." Art began laughing loudly.

Carl decided to take a gamble, he had a hunch. "Guess I won't get paid then."

"There's nobody left alive to pay you is there? Tony Inman probably died years ago and some Swiss bank will inherit all of the money. Let me tell you about this case of yours Carl. The two scumbags took their money to America where Inman was in charge of investing it. But he ran off with it instead, being the disloyal piece of shit that he is. His heartbroken sidekick Victor Boyle found himself without money or leadership. The moron spends the rest of his sordid life chasing after it, even hires you as a last resort. Then with you on the case he dies on the street like a dog. Maybe you should come with a health warning."

"Guess so."

"Why are you here fishing for information? Your client is dead on a slab at the morgue. Don't you have anybody's wandering wife to follow?"

Carl pretended to be reluctant to speak. Made it appear that he was not sure what to do. Art was from the agency and was trained to spot a lie. Lies typically flow so Carl knew that his one couldn't. After appearing to wrestle with his better judgment Carl made his move.

"I spoke to Victor Boyle last week shortly before he was shot and he told me that you were the third man." Carl was dragging Graham Greene into the game now. It seemed apt.

"Third man? What's a motherfucking third man mean?"

"He said that you were their partner in Saigon. That you were in the Phoenix Program together, that and a few extortion rackets on the side and all that kind of stuff. He said that you recommended him to hire me. Would have liked to do it yourself but you told him you couldn't because we didn't get on."

He was bright red, beyond angry. In spite of all his training he was about to fall into Carl's trap with a little help from his own arrogance.

"Me their fucking partner? Me? I fucking hated them! They had a partner, Colonel Bao from Vietnamese intelligence. He had a share of their money until his car blew up a few weeks before Saigon fell. My best friend investigated their activities in Nam and pointed out that they arrested an unusual number of young girls they claimed were working for the communists. None of these girls were ever seen again after Inman and Boyle had their fun with them. A day after he showed his superiors the math was off the scale and didn't add up, his car blew up with him in it. This was just days before the fall of Saigon when he would have gone home to his wife and children in Houston alive instead of in pieces in a motherfucking body bag. Fucking Inman and Boyle were the biggest scumbags in the whole of South Vietnam. They were into every racket that they could find. They made millions before they left the agency. Inman supposedly ran off with at least twenty-million dollars and the idiot Boyle spent the rest of his life looking for him. Fucking good thing Boyle is dead or I would kill him myself! Me? Their motherfucking partner? Fucking scumbags!" He was contorting his face and spitting saliva as he spoke the last words.

Carl smiled to let him know that he had got what he wanted from him. Art realised what had happened and that Carl had made him lose his temper on purpose. Instead of continuing to be angry he became calm and smiled at Carl.

"What are you really up to Carl? You are not writing a history book on Vietnam I assume?"

"Working on staying alive Art. Mostly I'm just working on staying alive. Your friend was a good investigator. Focus on the young girls Art. You'll be able to work out the rest from there."

Carl paid his bill and was getting up to leave. Carl was the centre of attention and all the barflies were interested in the man who had taken on their hero and was still standing.

"If Inman is really out there and knows you are after him staying alive won't be easy. Take care of yourself Carl and don't start your car without looking under the hood first."

"Thanks Art," Carl said as he stood up and

paid his bill.

As he passed Art on his way out he heard him speak into his drink so quietly that only Carl could hear.

"Get that scumbag for me Carl. If he is still alive somebody better nail him. Like permanently, for all the widows and orphans."

"Don't forget the grieving parents Art. There are a lot of them too," Carl said with his back to the audience passing Art at the bar as he pushed through the door into the morning sunlight.

Carl had got what he wanted. He had found out where Victor Boyle fitted into the story and, maybe more importantly, that Boyle had probably been Inman's sidekick in his murder games. He assumed that Boyle had needed a leader and couldn't pursue his sport without the senior partner. It begged the question as to what Boyle had missed the most. Had he spent twenty years chasing the money or had he wanted back into Inman's murder games? Things had started to get interesting. The case was not only about a serial killer; it was also about money, lots and lots of money. Carl would stick with it no matter what. Just because he sometimes believed in good old-fashioned justice didn't mean that he was above the money.

CHAPTER 14

It was time for another drink and he needed a safe place where he could sit and think. There was another bar he had used to drink at a little further along Suriwongse Road called Candy's and it was usually open. Carl briskly walked the hundred meters there. Candy's didn't look open to the people passing by and only the handful of people who knew the place well would bother to try the door. As usual the door was unlocked so Carl opened it and went inside.

There were seven members of staff in the bar looking half asleep, and Bob the Australian owner was sitting at the end of the bar on his own. On his left shoulder, as always, was a large white bird that walked backwards and forwards staring angrily around the bar with dark beady eyes. The bird was called Ned Kelly and was famous for his ability to say 'suck my dick' in several languages.

Two of the youngest girls were still wearing their pink pyjamas and had faces smeared with talcum powder. These two teenagers were sitting at the sofa furthest inside the bar and near the door to the toilet. This was also the door to the upper floors where the girls slept on mats on the floor. They were eating rice and an assortment of spicy strong smelling things from several plastic plates, picking the food up with rice they had pressed into balls with their hands. The bar was also where they lived.

Two of the older girls in their day clothes got up from the nearest sofa and walked to the bar where Carl was sitting himself down. These would be the two that hadn't made any money the night before. The girls liked to spread money around so everybody got a chance when they were hungry. There was less fighting that way. Cat-fights between bar girls were not a pleasant spectacle.

"About time you put in an appearance," Bob, the owner, said to Carl.

Bob was a thin man from some angles. He had a long face and skinny arms and legs. His belly had betrayed him and was another story. He had the hugely distended middle of a man who had spent most of his existence drinking for a living. As usual he was badly dressed in the cheap copy clothing that was sold in the Patpong night market. Carl wondered how he was able to buy clothing from Patpong as Bob lived upstairs in an apartment on the top floor and, as far as Carl was aware, hadn't left the building in years. Maybe he sent one of his staff out to buy his clothes. Somebody was obviously robbing him. The clothes he was wearing were the cheapest looking Carl had ever seen. Maybe Bangkok had copied the copies.

"How's business?" Carl asked him.

"Sydney or the bush, mate," he replied in Australian.

"Like always then."

"Fuckin' right, mate."

"Where's the old mamasan?" Carl asked. The old mamasan had worked for Bob and looked after him and his staff for over ten years.

"Some bloke who made loads of money working the mines in Australia came in, rooted her rotten and buggered her senseless, so she married him. He was my best customer and I really miss him," Bob said laughing loudly. "They bought a house in Pattaya and filled it with sex toys from eBay."

"Glad to see romance is still alive and well and living at Candy's bar."

"My bloody oath. They should call me Cupid. It is fucking hard to run a business when the silly cows keep falling for the customers and running off and marrying them. If you knew how many marriages this place is responsible for," Bob said, minus his laugh. "Do you know Carl, every man, no matter how old, ugly, or stupid he is, has some silly cow somewhere that is just waiting for him to walk up to her so she can fall in love with him?"

"Guess that means we will eventually be all right then Bob."

"Women! Don't bloody understand them."

The girls started massaging Carl's arms in the hope that he would buy them a drink. The problem was he couldn't even hold a drink as his arms were being held firmly by the massaging girls. He ordered drinks anyway, one for him and one for each of the girls.

"Sorry to hear about your car," Bob told him.

"What about my car?" Carl asked.

"There were two plain clothes policemen in here last night looking for you. They said they needed to let you know that someone had crashed into your Porsche in a Patpong car park."

"What did you tell them?" Carl asked in a put-on calm voice.

"I told them the truth, that I hadn't seen you in almost a year."

"Then what happened?"

"They buggered off of course. I don't like police in my bar."

"Were they in uniform?"

"No, mate, like I said, undercover blokes. Safari suits with a bulge at the waistband. You know; carrying heat."

"If they come back don't say you saw me."

"You in trouble, mate?"

"Pissed off some rich bastard by shagging his wife," Carl lied fluently.

"So nothing new then, sport," he said with great amusement.

Carl moved one of the girl's hands to his back so he had a free hand to lift his drink. Carl felt the need to drink come over him again as he had been given yet another thing to think about. He had been feeling the need to drink a lot lately. One of the girls smiled at him and moved her hand down to massage his balls. They could rub him anywhere they liked as long as they kept their hands off the pockets with the stacks of money in them.

"Do you want a blow-job?" she whispered in his ear.

Carl imagined himself with his trousers around his ankles, back to the wall and facing the door as his hunters crashed into the bar. It wasn't so much the thought of a shootout whilst half naked that bothered him. What really worried him was being posthumously infamous. Carl imagined the headline, 'The Stiff with a Stiffy' or 'He Died with his Boots On' or 'Private Detective Blown Away'. It was vanity but that was really not how Carl wanted to be remembered.

"I can't," Carl told her, "I am a Rotarian."

"You can," she replied hungrily, "all the other Rotarians do. They come here every Thursday afternoon."

There was no answer to that so he ignored the original question. He might change his mind after a few drinks anyway. Your reputation becomes less important when you are drunk, or so he had heard. The trick was to keep drinking and talking normally in spite of his erection, not always an easy thing to do as her hand was massaging all the right parts. So Carl thought about a bullet in the back of the head and ordered everybody another drink.

"What I always wanted to ask you is how did you find that gang last year?" Bob asked. "Four days wasn't it, that it took you to find them?"

"I did what I always do Bob."

"And what's that, mate?"

"I stuck a pin in a map," Carl said with a grin.

"Fuck you," Bob said angrily.

"I thought that was her job," Carl replied nodding his head in the direction of the girl that was making eyes at him whilst rubbing his dick and balls.

The owner pointed at a sign behind the cashier's head. It said, 'Whores are people that do well for money what other people do badly for love.' He laughed out loud again at his own wit.

"No chance you will be getting married then," Carl told him.

"My bloody oath mate. But seriously, I want to know how you find people that nobody else can find."

Carl thought for a while before he answered. "I think it is more empathy, more getting my hands dirty and a lot less Hollywood than other investigators."

"I still don't get it," were Bob's final words regarding the matter. He had resigned himself to being a brothel keeper and accepted that he would never reach the dizzy lows of being a Bangkok private inquiry agent.

Bob had the life he wanted. He owned a bar around the corner from Patpong. He got drunk with his friends every night and could always find a woman or two to look after him in his drunken stupors. He thought he was in heaven. Maybe he was, but then why did so many people in his line of work drink themselves to death? Carl always wondered if they brought the unhappiness with them or picked it up later. Carl occasionally liked visiting the Patpong life but had long ago stopped wanting to live there.

"Speaking of marriage Carl," Bob said, laughing again, "When are you planning your next famous disaster?"

"I'm done with marriage. It would be doomed to failure anyway. I don't like Pattaya and I don't have an eBay account."

"You're better off single mate. There's lots of perks to being free. Take little Ann there, she can suck start a Harley Davidson and she never says no to anybody."

"I will bear that in mind."

Meanwhile, it was decision time, and Carl didn't want to walk out onto the main street with an erection. He gave the girls a hundred baht each and thanked them. It was a polite way of saying, 'get your hands off me please'. He asked for the bill hoping it wouldn't arrive too quickly. He needed time to get back to normal before he walked out into the daylight.

His erection problem was solved. It was immediately demolished when Bart Barrows crashed through the door and took a seat next to him at the bar. The two girls in pink pyjamas had gone upstairs, the other two were eating at the table they had vacated, and the only remaining girls were gathered around Carl.

"What's going on here Bob and what's that white bird?" Bart asked as the bartender put his brand of beer in front of him.

"You know what it is. It's a cockatoo," Bob told him.

"Pity it's not a cunt or two or you might be doing some business in here," Bart barked as he looked around the bar unhappily.

"That's all right, it's your lucky day. I was just leaving," Carl told Bart, who sipped on a bottle of beer, relieved that he was not going to be sitting alone for long.

"You leaving already, mate?" Bob asked unhappily, which was understandable as Carl was his best customer so far that day. Bart Barrows could make a bottle of beer last a very long time.

"Got to go back to the office," Carl lied. He didn't have an office.

"Remember, work is the curse of the drinking class," Bob told him as he pointed at another sign behind the bar, this one quoting Oscar Wilde.

"How can I forget?" Carl told him as he left.

The street looked safe but Carl was understandably paranoid. He walked back into Patpong and went through the first open door, a Thai restaurant on the South side of the street. These places all had back doors that came out onto a lane that ran behind Patpong. He made sure he wasn't followed in and then left by the back door making sure that he wasn't followed out. There was nobody shadowing him so he relaxed and walked along the alley back toward Suriwongse Road. He was in a high stakes game and like all games it was fun as long as you were winning.

Carl performed a few more counter surveillance tricks and then took a taxi back to Sukhumvit. He got out of the taxi at the entrance to one of the many tall office buildings that line Soi Asoke, the main thoroughfare that runs from Sukhumvit to Phetchburi Road. Carl took the lift to the 24th floor where Damien Southerby's supposedly secret office was located.

On the 24th floor there was a security door that the Israeli Embassy would have been proud of and a security camera that watched the whole area between the lift and the reinforced door. Carl looked into the camera and pressed the buzzer. He waited, and waited, and then Carl waited some more. He imagined the hyper paranoid activity that would have been going on the other side of the door. He was fully aware that Damien did not approve of visitors and his unexpected arrival would cause him much distress. Fifteen minutes later the door opened and Damien was standing in front of Carl with a strained and curious expression on his face.

"What're you doing here and how the fuck did you know where it was?" Damien asked him.

"I just followed the twinkle of diamond cufflinks. Now, let me in and give me some coffee. I have a problem you can help me with Damien."

Damien waved his hand for Carl to follow him. As Carl entered, the door automatically shut itself behind him. The inside of the office was bigger than he had expected. The main floor was open plan except for partitions, desks and headsets that were linked to electronic boxes. The boxes provided access to the Internet for the crowd of spotty youths to make their long distance phone calls. The noise reminded Carl of a large flock of geese as one hundred bonus-driven men, some sitting and some standing, yelled into their headsets trying to find the next deal.

Carl had imagined that these latter-day snake oil salesmen would spend their days sweet-talking little old ladies into investing in their rigged foreign exchange program. The reality was aggressive salesmen screaming abuse at dentists, doctors, architects and other professional types sitting at their desks in legitimate offices on the other side of the world.

As Carl walked past the badly dressed, overpaid runaways from their small towns in America, Europe and Australia, Carl heard things like "Who wears the fucking trousers in your house?" and "Call yourself a man?" and "You have to grow balls to make money" and Carl's all-time favourite, "I am going out in my Ferrari tonight to drink Champagne and fuck models two at a time. What are you doing tonight?"

Damien led Carl across the full length of the telemarketing floor to his office. The door closed behind them and there was silence. Damien's office was soundproofed and separated from the outside world by thick floor to ceiling glass. Damien could play Fagin in peace whilst keeping a close eye on his room full of Dickensian urchins.

"What do you think?" he asked Carl.

"I think I should have learnt to pick a pocket or two."

"I rarely understand what you are talking about. You are good at your job with a tendency toward simplification, which I appreciate. However, when I talk to you on other matters I never know what the fuck you are talking about."

"I've a problem understanding myself most of the time too. Shall we get down to business?"

"OK. What brings you here scaring the shit

out of my staff? Fuck, we thought we were being raided. I swear my star salesman's pissed his pants."

"Sorry about that but I don't have a lot of time. I need an anonymous offshore structure with a virgin bank account attached. I need it now so there is no time for lawyers. I know you will need backup bank accounts in your back pocket at all times to replace the ones shut down by the authorities as they become aware of your activities. I am guessing that bank accounts are getting shut down all the time so you will always be in possession of at least three corporate structures and three virgin bank accounts."

"You know far too much," Damien said unhappily.

"That's why you like me Damien. Anyone else would be here to extort money from you. I'm here to ask for a favour and pay a fair price in cash on the table for it. I need the bank account, preferably in a morally loose jurisdiction, with all passwords and security devices. I will pay you cash now for whatever it originally cost you to set up and, and should I be successful in my endeavour, I will give you a very serious Patek Philippe watch as a gift from me to you, it will be a mark of friendship. I won't insult you by offering you money I know you don't need. But Damien, a man can never have too many beautiful watches, plus there are times in everybody's life when a friend like me can be worth a lot more than money."

Damien smiled. "What's this endeavour of yours Carl? That's a very expensive gift you are offering me."

"It is for a client and my confidentiality was guaranteed in the package as always. Can you help me with this matter Damien? Time's of the essence."

"I should have what you need lying about here somewhere."

"That is a great weight off my mind. Now, Damien, where's that fucking coffee you cheapskate? And none of that powdered crap please."

Damien picked up the phone on his desk and asked for two coffees to be sent in with the file on a company called Mayfair Assets. They both sat waiting for the coffee to arrive with huge grins on their faces like two naughty schoolboys who were in the process of getting away with something big.

CHAPTER 15

The crocodile was meandering down the fifteenth fairway. Crocodile was the name the Thais gave to the unusually large group of caddies and security men that made a long and twisted shape as it followed the biggest of shots whenever they played golf. As usual this crocodile was made up of caddies carrying golf bags, caddies with umbrellas, caddies holding fold-up chairs, caddies who were only there because they were pretty, and armed men sweating in dark safari suits holding two-way radios. Six men were playing slow gambling golf and holding up all the smaller unimportant groups that had become jammed up on the holes behind them. The golf courses didn't allow six players in a group but this was Thailand and the generals did whatever they wanted.

Anthony Inman was walking beside General Amnuay and they had separated from the rest of the group. They always spoke Thai to each other even though General Amnuay's English was fluent American.

"Did you have to kill Victor, he was our friend once if you can remember?" General Amnuay asked. "It made a lot of noise. Now the embassy will want a proper *investigation."*

"*He had to go. More importantly the private detective has to go as soon as possible.*"

"*Why? Do you owe him money too?*" *Amnuay stopped walking and laughed loudly at his own joke.*

"*Look here.*" *Inman stopped beside him and spoke strongly. "This Carl Engel idiot is a threat to all of us and he has to die now.*"

"*You mean he is a threat to you. He can't hurt me.*"

"*As you say, I need him dead.*"

General Amnuay massaged his own face with his right hand. Then he half closed one eye and said, "I have given you the Cat and the Rat to take orders directly from you. They can kill anybody you need killed, even your old friends, so what's the problem?"

"*They can't find him. I need access to Special Branch again.*"

"*Special Branch can't be used for now. Since the coup everybody is trying to spy on everybody else. Even Special Branch is being watched so they will only act in their official capacity until things get back to normal.*"

"*How can I find this man then?*" *Inman asked unhappily.*

"*The Cat and the Rat have their own contacts. He is only a farang, there is no reason they won't be able to find him.*"

"*This farang has been here thirty-five years.*"

"*They are Thai, he is only farang. Of course they can find him.*"

"*I have already cancelled a shipment because of him.*

180

He is costing us a lot of money," Inman said in a last ditch effort to get General Amnuay's full attention.

"Maybe if you stopped playing your games with the young girls our business would run more smoothly," the general said and then walked off to find his ball.

Anthony Inman waited for his caddy to catch up, took a five-iron from her, and hit his ball cleanly the remaining one hundred and ninety yards onto the green. He smiled knowing he was in the perfect position to win another hole.

Carl needed to use his Blackberry with his original phone number and list of contacts. It felt like paranoia as he took a taxi to the Thonburi side of the river. Carl knew his enemies were no phantoms and their brief was to put a bullet in his head, so wasting several hours being elaborately careful didn't feel like a total waste of time.

The other side of the river is different to the Bangkok side. It is like a foreign country and they do things differently there. Carl had asked the taxi driver, much to his amusement, to drive around Thonburi for ten minutes and then take him back over the bridge.

He switched on his Blackberry and it started coughing out beeps as it downloaded messages. There were several e-mails that were not of interest, as he was not taking on any new cases. There were the usual messages from friends asking where he was and did he want to meet up for a beer. There was a message from Duke's saying people had been in there asking about him. If they were concerned enough to let him know by SMS then they hadn't liked the look of the people who were doing the asking. There was also a message from Jack, the head of security at the Sukhumvit Grande. He was in a funk because one of his guests had been murdered. Fear took its grip and made Carl feel physically unwell and uncoordinated.

It was logical to assume that Carl was being treated as a missing persons investigation and would be searched for by the standard methods. The trouble was he didn't think that they were planning to serve papers on him, arrest him, or tap him on the shoulder and tell him he needed to call home. The people doing the hunting were, he assumed, the same people who had gunned down Victor Boyle. Their brief would be the same, get rid of Carl before he talked to too many people. Inman wanted the toothpaste put back in the tube and didn't care how messy it got.

Carl needed a cigarette. He asked the taxi to pull over and park by the side of the road for a while. Carl stood on the pavement smoking. A foolish habit but compared to how he lived the rest of his life it seemed sane enough. He called the colonel from the pavement.

"Where have you been?" The colonel sounded annoyed. "I can't reach you on your phone."

"The fat man outside the Sheraton was my

client and now the same people are looking for me."

"Okay. What do you need?"

"I need a meeting. Somewhere safe. How about that place we met the informant during the Nigerian case a few years ago?"

"What time?"

"Three o'clock. Don't think I'm being paranoid but make sure you are not followed."

"I won't be," he told Carl. "I had a strange phone call this morning from a policeman that I don't know. He said they needed you to do some translation work for them and could I put them in touch. I told them you owed me money and if they found you to let me know."

"I'll tell you what is going on at three," Carl said and disconnected.

After attaching the picture of the men standing behind him at the airport that he had received from George, and messaging it to the colonel, he switched off his Blackberry and got back in the taxi. Carl instructed the driver to take him back to the Bangkok side of the river and deliver him to Sukhumvit Soi 5. The meeting place he had chosen was a large sports pub and restaurant with food, drinks, pool tables, and big-screen televisions so it would be busy enough to feel anonymous in.

Carl got out of the taxi at the top of the street. Soi 5 was a narrow one-way street that became a horseshoe with Soi 7 going one way in the other direction and letting the cars get back to Sukhumvit Road. It had a supermarket, small hotels, and lots of bars. The top end of the street was a hangout for African pimps and drug dealers. Shopping at the supermarket was an unusual experience as you were likely to be whispered to by big African men with offers of ecstasy, cocaine, speed or if that was not your bag they would offer to get you a big African prostitute from around the corner. It was known in Bangkok as little Africa and the police looked the other way.

Carl walked along the street and ignored the yells of, "Hey man," from the groups of African males outside Foodland supermarket. Carl wasn't buying. He walked on a little way to the bar opposite the pub he was going to meet the colonel at and found a discreet corner where he could observe the comings and goings across the street. Carl trusted the colonel but did not know how good his pursuers were. He wasn't going in there until he knew the colonel hadn't been followed.

The colonel arrived promptly at three and he was on foot. He was obviously taking the situation very seriously. Not only had Carl never seen him arrive anywhere on time before but, more importantly, he had never seen him arrive anywhere without his Mercedes. He went into the pub, looked around, and when he couldn't find Carl he picked a discreet table in the corner and waited. He was in civilian clothes but still had his shiny police boots on. The boots were always the first thing people noticed. Everywhere he went they knew he was a policeman. Maybe that was the point.

Carl watched for the next ten minutes until he was sure the colonel hadn't been followed. If he had, Carl was confident that he would have seen them. In such a small street there were a limited number of positions they could have used to watch what was happening in the pub, and from where Carl was he could see all of them. Feeling reassured he crossed the street, went inside and sat down at the table.

"So tell me what this is about," the colonel said almost in a whisper.

Carl told him everything, the whole story. The only part that brought a smile to the colonel's face was how Carl had gone through old direct mailing lists to confirm Inman's presence in Thailand under the then known alias. Apart from that his face remained deadly serious throughout.

"You are in trouble this time," he told Carl. "You no longer have a client and anything you do will be seen as a direct attack by this man and his associates. You will not be a service provider, you will be the enemy."

"Quite."

"I did a check on his mobile phone. He has some powerful friends in the police and the army. He makes a lot of calls to General Amnuay."

General Amnuay was the army's equivalent of a godfather. He had a reputation of being involved in most of the profitable rackets. As far as Carl knew, he didn't have a lot of enemies, not live ones anyway. The situation was getting worse on a daily basis.

"Did you get the picture I sent you? They are the ones that followed me from the airport."

"They are soldiers. I mean they were soldiers. They are well known to the police by their nicknames Cat and Rat. They are from a group of rogue Special Forces. They are Mafia for hire to politicians and big shots. They had promising military careers until they got exposed in an FBI case involving Americans smuggling guns to the Yakuza in Japan. They were the suppliers. The guns were being stolen from upcountry Army bases. They were never prosecuted but were kicked out of the Army instead. Now they make their living as muscle for hire."

"Did they ever get the boss? The one that would have fronted the money and had the overseas connections?"

"No. The FBI only got the mules. They were low rank US marines. They were the people that hand-carried the guns on US military flights to Japan. Nobody else was ever prosecuted."

"So if Inman was the man at the top it would explain why he has the friends that he does," Carl said.

"Let's assume that what you say is true and not another one of your colourful hypotheses. Your man plays golf with very powerful men and is their link to foreign gangsters overseas. He makes the deals and launders the money. This is not a man that you want as your enemy. This man can be fatal if you get in his way. This is all theory though so we need to focus on what we know to be fact."

"Point taken," Carl said reluctantly. "We know I was being followed and am now being searched for by ex-soldiers that kill their enemies."

"Yes."

"Any advice?"

"Don't let them find you."

He pushed something to Carl under the table. It was a gun. Carl didn't like guns.

"Keep this. It is untraceable to me. It was confiscated during a case and never got filed as evidence. Try not to get caught carrying it. I know you don't like guns but if these people find you you'll be glad you've got it."

Carl took it, pulled his shirt outside his trousers, and tucked the cold metal into the front of his belt. The shirt and his expanding belly would hide it.

"Did you find out anything about the student murders?" Carl asked.

"Not much that the newspapers are not already aware of, like the missing ears they put in every headline. The only thing the papers don't know yet is that all the murdered girls were active on computer dating sites. Not the 'will you marry me' ones, but the students looking to fuck a foreigner for money ones."

"You mean prostitutes?"

"Certainly not. They were not from poor families."

The colonel believed that only the rural poor were to be classed as true criminals. Anybody whose family owned anything in Bangkok larger than a shop house was just being clever when they profited from an illegal or immoral act. Clever people and the money they spent played an important part in the local economy.

Internet sex negotiation had become very big. It entailed explicit sexual conversations online with the intention of meeting for immediate sex. This enabled people to have sex with a stranger with less risk of embarrassment as the flirting process had already taken place. It also pre-qualified them as having similar sexual tastes.

As appealing as it occasionally sounded Carl had never tried it. There was a lack of something, romance probably. But more than that, Carl's awareness of the duality of people killed any possibility of taking strangers at face value. Every time he thought he was being unnecessarily judgmental, something, like dead people in morgues, would prevent him from changing his mind.

"Have they traced the last person any of the victims had been chatting to?"

"Not really. It can be very anonymous. A lot of the men are married so not posting a picture is quite normal. They did some Internet tracing but all they got was public wireless areas in shopping centres. If the killer had a device that he only used for this one purpose then there is no way of linking it back to him. Unless he logged on using it in his own home or place of work, which he didn't."

"But they believe that the killer is a foreigner?" Carl asked him.

"Either that or a Thai pretending to be a foreigner."

"No," Carl said with total certainty. "This killer is a foreigner."

"So what do you want me to do?"

"Can you point the investigators in the right direction? Tell them to look into Inman, I mean Somchai Poochokdee? I know he is the killer."

"What are you going to do?"

"I am going to avoid eating in busy restaurants."

"Apart from that?"

"I will work on gathering evidence that can later be passed on to the police."

"It won't be easy to get a proper investigation into a man that plays golf with the generals."

"If I prove he is killing teenage girls

somebody must be willing to lock him up," Carl said.

"How can you be so naive?" the colonel asked him angrily.

"That's always a good question."

"We've been here long enough," the colonel said as he stood up.

Carl agreed with him and they left the pub separately.

Late afternoon on busy lower Sukhumvit Road was probably not a good place for him to be. Carl cut through the backstreets from Soi 5 to Soi 3, an area that is known as the Arab Quarter as it was the centre for middle-eastern restaurants and cafes offering hubbly-bubbly pipes. He came out at the Nana intersection. An even worse place to be as it was where the popular Nana bars were. And at that time of day they would be full of foreigners that knew Carl.

A taxi was looking for a fare and Carl quickly slid in the backseat. He needed clothes so he told the taxi to take him to a department store on the other side of the river, Thonburi again. All Carl needed was a Levis outlet, and he would be able to find one at the old department store across the river. It was a long way to go in Bangkok traffic but he had nothing better to do. Carl had decided that he would give up shaving and wear nothing but blue jeans for a while.

CHAPTER 16

Carl was wearing the clean clothes he had put on at the department store. He dropped the rest of the shopping off at the room. The need for creature comforts had overruled common sense on the return journey and he had made the taxi stop at the Hyatt Hotel so he could buy books, a bottle of Ardbeg single malt, and a box of Cuban cigars. He was starting to feel himself again, to hell with enemies.

On his way out he slipped his man some more money and let him know there was luggage in the room, failing to mention that it was in paper and plastic shopping bags. The attendant didn't ask any questions or show any interest in what was going on. As long as he remembered to slip him some money every day Carl could have been screwing his way through a circus troupe, animals and all, or running an opium den for all the attendant cared.

By early evening Carl was sitting in one of Bangkok's famous and trendy bars. He was inconspicuous as his blue jeans and three-day beard were perfect camouflage amongst Bangkok's middle class drinkers. Brown Sugar was a jazz pub on the street that ran behind Lumpini Park. It had opened in the 1980s when Carl was a relatively young man and its murky and relaxed atmosphere where Thais and foreigners mingled was a novelty in the Bangkok of that time. It suited his mood that night as he craved something familiar. The frontage was mostly glass so Carl had gone straight to a table at the very back where there was the least light.

He had called George from the taxi and given him a cryptic clue to where he was going; the Rolling Stones like it in their coffee. He was confident that George would be able to solve it; he had taken great interest in Carl's daily battles with the Bangkok Post's cryptic crossword. George was reliable as always. Carl was only on his third beer when he arrived and sat down opposite him.

"I took the long way here to make sure I wasn't followed."

"I figured you would," Carl told him as he ordered him a beer.

"What is our present status?"

Carl placed a rolled up paper bag on the table in front of him.

"What is it?" George asked without picking it up.

"Spoils of war. Two-hundred-thousand Hong Kong dollars in cash that I need you to hide for me."

George wrinkled his brow, looked at the bag, looked at Carl and then slid it onto his lap.

"Do you have a plan or is this bohemian look permanent?" he asked, having taken note of the designer stubble and new wardrobe.

"Floundering a little," Carl told him. "Seems the colonel doesn't believe that telling the police our man is a serial killer is a prudent thing to do."

"Why would he say that?"

"Seems our target may be doing business and playing golf with General Amnuay. Information is that he may be a bit of a handful."

"Handful? The man is the biggest gangster in town. You have really got yourself in a mess again. How the hell do you plan to get out of this one?"

"That, George, is the question that murders sleep."

"I see a future with a very long beard if you don't think of something soon."

Carl was relieved to see he still had his sense of humour. A sense of humour goes a long way when surrounded by people who want you dead and possess the means.

"I want to pay a late night visit to Inman's old office building on Phetchburi Road," Carl told him. "Don't know where it fits in, but something about it isn't right. It is a very expensive piece of real estate to leave idle for so many years. Especially when you are in the real estate business. That and the fact that somebody is still paying the electricity bill."

"What's on your mind?"

"Do you still pick locks?"

"Sounds like I'll have to," he said wearily.

The plan was to go there late. Closing time, when the police were all busy dealing with the drunks. George left to put the money somewhere safe and Carl ordered a plate of food and slowed down his beer consumption. Getting comfortably numb on alcohol was always a temptation when dealing with stress but not a good idea before a burglary. The piped jazz music was pleasant enough but he wasn't in the mood.

The live music started at nine and the band typically showed up a little before. The band comprised a piano player, double bass, tenor saxophone, and a long-legged black vocalist. She was beautiful. Her name was Jacqueline, and once upon a time she had almost become another Mrs. Engel. When she saw him in the corner she came and sat in the seat George had recently vacated.

"It's been a long time Carl," she told him, looking at him with sparkling but disapproving eyes.

"Sounds like the title of a song. How've you been?"

"Tall, black, and beautiful mostly. How 'bout you?"

"Cynical, grumpy, and self-possessed. Same as

always."

"No wonder you're so irresistible to women."

"Do you still sing Misty in your sleep?"

"How would I know? Who's around to tell me?" she said as she signalled the waiter for a drink. "The Dutchman comes here regularly, he told me that you are back. Why didn't you come and see me?"

"I didn't think you'd want me to."

"That's your most annoying trait, always thinking. Real life is such a mystery to you. I could never work out whether you are an idiot genius or a genius at being an idiot."

"Me too. I thought about calling you, but eh, you know me."

"Yeah I know you. Forgiving everybody except yourself. I have to go and sing, will you be around later?" she asked as she leant over and kissed Carl on the cheek. She picked up her drink and walked away without waiting for an answer.

Carl missed her more than he liked to admit. The relationship was not going to be warmed up by him under his present circumstances and he couldn't tell her why without making her an accomplice. She was going to be handled at arm's length for a while. Being close to him immediately shaved decades off a person's life expectancy and she sang far too well to die young. Like dodgem cars that crashed and passed in the night, Carl knew another wedge had just been put between them.

They had only ever had one argument but one had been enough. She had asked Carl what it had been like living in Thailand as a young foreigner during the 1970s and 1980s. He told her that it had been like being a Negro in a Swiss village in wintertime. She was offended and declared it a racist statement. Carl disagreed and told her that racism would be behaving and speaking differently when she was around and that he had no intention of putting a governor between his thoughts and his mouth. She gave Carl a lecture on American style political correctness. Carl insisted that political correctness was just an insidious form of racism, as it required putting on different behaviour for different people. They did not agree and her programming had kicked in. She remained angry with him for quite some time after. Carl could put up with almost anything, but not her disapproval. So he had gone quietly.

She stood in front of the grand piano and sang Misty. She sang the words to him across the crowded bar as if it was only the two of them there. Just like the old days when he used to pick her up at the Brown Sugar late at night. She didn't sing at Carl again all night and didn't come back and talk to him. After taking time to think about what she had said, Carl's money was on just plain 'idiot'. He would do what he had to do and then go to bed with his bottle of Ardbeg. A marriage made in heaven.

Once, she had confided to the Dutchman that she reckoned some woman had broken Carl's heart, and how she would like to get her hands on that woman for ruining him for everybody else. The Dutchman said, 'no, no, no,' and told her that it was not a woman that had drawn first blood. It was life that had broken Carl's heart but that had been a very long time ago. The Dutchman's theory, he had claimed, was based on something he had heard Carl say in India whilst wasted on hashish and booze. Carl thought they were both talking nonsense but then, what did he know?

George got back around midnight and spent a few minutes huddled at a table with Jacqueline. They openly conspired whilst unashamedly glancing in Carl's direction. They had long ago joined forces believing two heads would be better than one at unravelling the enigma that was their common burden. Carl always let them have their fun; two martyrs were definitely better than one. He paid the bill and waited.

George had brought a discreet midsize Japanese car with him that Carl didn't recognise and thought it best not to ask about. George got in the driver's seat and drove the car towards their destination in silence. The traffic was only medium weight even though some of the bars had already begun to send their customers home. The cold gun pressed against Carl's belly was disturbing but uncharacteristically comforting. As usual, Carl hoped he knew what he was doing.

The car park behind the building was quiet as the grave. The shop houses around the square were all shut for the night. There was nobody to be seen but Carl assumed that some of the people would live above their businesses so windows were relevant and they needed to be careful. They parked the car behind the building and George switched off the headlights.

"What's next?" he asked Carl. "Was it your turn to bring the ladder?"

"Sad story George. The ladder's in the pawn shop again."

"Does that mean we can go home now?"

"We have the advantage of being old and respectable foreigners," Carl told him. "Being furtive would make us conspicuous whereas walking up to the door and opening it like we own the place shouldn't draw any attention whatsoever."

"I assume this wonderful plan is based on my ability to pick the lock so quickly it will appear like we have a key," he said sarcastically.

"If you're as quick with a lock as you are quick witted then I have nothing to worry about," Carl said smiling. "Walk over, stop near the door and light a cigarette so you can know what we're up against."

"I don't smoke."

"That makes two foolish acts you get to

perform in one night. Or is it already three? Do we count car theft?" Carl said as he handed George a cigarette and a lighter.

George got out of the car and walked straight as if he was going to pass the door. He stopped and spent a long time in the shadow of the back of the building performing a wonderful act of trying to light a cigarette with a lighter that kept going out. He gave up after several attempts and resumed his walk away from the car. A few minutes later he had doubled back around the building and was back in the driver's seat. He handed Carl back the lighter.

"I can pop that lock in reasonable time," he told Carl as he reached into the glove compartment for a torch.

"Let's do it then."

George put the torch in his pocket and they got out of the car. They both walked confidently up to the back door and George got to work on the lock. It seemed much longer to Carl than the minute he actually took to open it. Then they were inside. George switched on the torch and they began to explore the building.

The ground floor was four shop houses wide and one of the four had a large metal roll-down shutter that opened to the pavement of the main road. These rusty roll-down doors were standard on shop houses all over Bangkok. The rest of the front of the building across three units was floor to ceiling glass. Inside the metal shutter there were tire marks on the dusty floor surrounded by footprints of various sizes. Only one set of footprints appeared to be male. Someone had been parking their car on the ground floor recently and he had been bringing guests with small feet.

They took the open stairs against the wall up to the second floor where there was a large teak door leading into what had obviously been the boss's office. The door was heavily ornate and the room behind it was very large, taking up most of the entire second floor. There were well made wooden shelves and cabinets behind a place that a very large desk would have once been. It looked like an ordinary deserted office building until you looked closer, and there was an unusual metallic smell to the air. Carl took George's hand and directed the torch around the room.

"Shit. He kills them here George. This is where it happens," Carl whispered. His knees were trembling and his voice was shaking.

"What do you see?" George asked him in a whisper.

"The windows have two layers of curtain, light reflective silver underneath and thick black curtain material so no one can see in when they are closed. The windows are more recent than the rest of the structure, very expensive thick double-glazing. The bathroom in the corner has all the requirements for taking a thorough shower. If you look at the walls and door they are soundproofed. And, just up there, where I am pointing the torch there is a metal ring attached to the wall, strong enough to restrain somebody. The brown patches on the wall are probably dried blood, see how it is smeared and pale brown like somebody tried to wash it off. You recognise that metallic smell George. This whole place smells like an abattoir."

"I've seen places like this in Vietnam," he whispered. "This is an evil place."

"Very evil indeed. Did you notice that all the female footprints point in the direction of this room? There are none pointing back downstairs. I want to get out of here, I think I've seen enough."

"Me too."

Carl took a quick look in the bathroom and noted the heavy duty cleaning fluids. Under the sink he saw a pile of rags, abrasive cleaning cloths, duct tape and a roll of black plastic sheet. Beside that was a box of tools and knives. Above the sink and under the mirror there was a box of Bolivar Churchill cigars. Carl opened it and with the light from the torch counted that sixteen cigars were gone.

"Fuck! Either he is a chain smoker or he has had a lot of victims in here."

"I hope he is a chain smoker," George said.

"Unfortunately I doubt that. There have been at least three rooms like this. There was one in America, one in Vietnam and now this one. Our devil is probably one of the most prolific serial killers of all time."

They both retreated very carefully smearing their footprints in the dust as they went backwards down the stairs. They had a quick last look before they left the building. There was nothing more to see but they had seen more than enough.

Back in the car George said, "I didn't really believe all this until just now."

"We can stop whispering now, George," Carl told him so he would appear more in control than he really felt. "I didn't totally believe it either. Now it is real, horribly real, and for some strange reason fate has made it our problem." Carl spoke softly, which was only slightly louder than a whisper.

"What the fuck do we do now Carl?" He said as softly.

"Go back to my room. There is a decent bottle of whisky there. We need to talk this through."

George very carefully, annoyingly slowly, drove the car past the building and out onto the main road. It was as if he was trying not to wake the ghosts. Carl didn't mind. He didn't want to wake them either.

CHAPTER 17

They went back to Carl's short-time room and opened the bottle of Ardbeg. The adrenalin was pumping so hard that the neat whisky tasted like water. George was sitting on the bed and Carl was in the room's only chair. They poured themselves another shot from the bottle on the bedside table before either of them spoke. They had not said a word throughout the drive back, not even when they stopped at a 7/11 store and Carl had jumped out to buy bottled water and cigarettes.

George opened the conversation. "What do we actually know about General Amnuay?"

Outside the room they could hear car engines, doors slamming and drunken arguments between people who did not speak the same languages. There was laughter too as a lot of the working girls enjoy themselves as much as the customers. Thais love a party. The Russian prostitutes are very different to the local girls though. From somewhere close to the door of their room they heard the cold professional accent from that part of the world telling an Italian who hardly spoke any English that, with the Russian girls, it was always money up front and she didn't care how the Thai girls did it.

"Amnuay is a very scary character," Carl said as he sipped his whisky. "The army's Mr. Big of the underworld. He is rumoured to be behind illegal casinos, massage parlours, drugs, and now we can assume, gun running to Japan. I read once that the heavyweight politicians and certain men in uniform have their own camps for housing assassins, hitmen's holiday homes. They use these camps to hide the assassins from the authorities between jobs. The article was written at the height of the Red Shirt and Yellow Shirt conflict when people were telling journalists things that are historically never spoken of in Thailand. It sounded very credible at the time," Carl said softly as, if they could hear the comings and goings from outside, then the people outside could hear them too.

"I didn't think the people that tailed you from the airport were boy scouts," George replied, also speaking softly. "They had the empty eyes of men that have killed without personal motive."

"They weren't police either. They are ex-soldiers that got caught running guns to the Yakuza on behalf of Amnuay and Inman."

"Why aren't they in prison then?" George asked.

"Because nobody in Thailand went to prison,

the only men charged were US marines that smuggled the guns on military flights between countries. The ones that got caught red-handed. Even though the case was thoroughly investigated by the FBI and the US military police, none of Amnuay's people were touched. That shows the power such men wield. The ex-soldiers that are looking for me have become guns for hire. The colonel described them as Ronin."

"He watches too many movies."

"General Amnuay is a lousy enemy to make. I have avoided crossing paths with people like him all of my life. I hoped men like him would never even know my name. He makes the situation a little too complex for my liking."

"Could you reason with him? Do what you usually do and send someone you know of military rank to talk to him on your behalf?"

"I have no value in his eyes so there is nothing to negotiate with," Carl replied.

"Maybe we can bypass him and just focus on Inman."

"Trouble is people like Inman with money and powerful friends don't go to prison in Thailand. The only wealthy people that are in prison are the ones that offended the aristocracy. Apart from that, Thailand is a perfect democracy. Perfect in that everybody does whatever they want to do and gets away with it. Apart from the poor but nobody counts them."

"I think some of the victims were from relatively middle-class families."

"Nobody takes the middle-class particularly seriously either," Carl replied.

"What are we?"

"Middle-bohemian George, definitely middle-bohemian. And none of them like us," Carl said with a hint of a smile.

George went to the bathroom and Carl poured them both another drink. When in doubt, get drunk. There was a fight somewhere outside the room. From what Carl could work out, one of the girls was beating up a verbally abusive customer. Then more voices as people arrived to break up the fight. Carl didn't object to the noise. He found noise comforting in his situation. When they came for him he knew there would be nothing but silence.

When George came out of the bathroom he said, "Do you have a plan yet?"

"Maybe," Carl said sitting back down in the chair. "Obviously we need to nail Inman. If we show the world what he is, all his big friends will have to turn their back on him. They have to, no matter how much money and old CIA business is on the table."

"His goose is cooked then. He is just a very old and vile foreign criminal and you've buried enough of them in your time," George said hopefully.

"That's entirely the wrong attitude," Carl replied. "It is extremely dangerous to belittle your enemy. It leads to unpleasant surprises and, what is worse, it removes all of the justification for fighting them in the first place. We must not underestimate this man. He's obviously insane but unfortunately he is not stupid. Quite the opposite in fact."

"So how do we start?" George asked.

Carl was glad George was feeling committed. Carl was a loner but this was not a time that he wanted to be alone. "Well we know where the killings are being done now. There will be DNA everywhere. Unfortunately an investigation into a foreigner in Thailand is never subtle. In fact, it is like a herd of elephants paying you a visit if you know what to look for. Inman will know the signs. He will soon know if he is being investigated."

"So he could destroy the evidence," George suggested.

"Worse than that. He would use General Amnuay's boys to hinder or stop any police investigation. He can certainly intimidate the newspapers enough for them to ignore the story. Once the phone calls started we would never motivate anyone to look at Inman again."

"You make it sound very bleak."

"It is fucking bleak George but continue we must. Do you remember old Mike from Glasgow?"

"The horrible alcoholic journalist that I can't understand a word he says? That Mike?"

"That's the one. He has been known to go against the local paper's policy of self-censorship and say what he thinks. If he could write about the murders from the stance of police incompetence and how a foreign serial killer is getting away with murder in Thailand, it may just stir up the necessary hornets' nest."

"Then what?"

"Then when the police are defending themselves and claiming it isn't true we, with a little help from my friends, declare Inman the prime suspect to the media at the Foreign Correspondents Club," Carl said confidently.

"You think that will work?"

"No I don't. Not as a solution to the real problem but it will get him off my back for a while. I am hoping he will be too busy sticking fingers in dikes to worry about me and once the cat is out of the bag I will no longer have the sole possession of the information that makes it necessary to kill me. If it's public knowledge I become less important."

"I know most of what you know," George said.

"I suggest we make sure nobody else knows that fact. I will go and talk to Mad Mike tomorrow morning, I mean this morning."

"Do you know him well?"

"He was a mourner at two of my weddings," Carl replied.

"What do you want me to do?"

"We need some sleep, we can get about four hours by my calculation. Then, in the morning I want you to find us a safe house. Somewhere we will not be found. This place is too horrible to lie low in."

There was a knock on the door and Carl signalled George to open it as he put his hand on the gun still tucked in the front of his jeans. Carl's man walked in, much to Carl's relief, as he felt too tired and drunk to shoot anybody. The man looked around the room and then sat himself down uninvited on the bed facing Carl. As always he spoke Thai to Carl. He began by apologising about the fight that had happened just outside the door and said he hoped it had not disturbed them. Carl told him it hadn't. Then the man leant forward and said, "Do you want girls? I have nice girls, very young and all the way from Chiangmai. These girls are very white skinned, the best." He was assuming that because Carl spoke Thai, his taste in women, or rather, in young girls, would be Asian.

"No thank you, we are a little too drunk tonight," Carl told him.

"These girls are very skilled and pretty, they can do whatever you ask. They can even make a drunken man happy. They haven't been working for long and they don't have many hairs yet. They are new enough to the work that they still feel a sexual need, if you know what I mean."

Carl knew that these girls would be

permanently based in the short-time hotel. They would have been bought and paid for in the North and brought to Bangkok as brothel workers. Many of the older short-time hotels also functioned as brothels. This was the sex slave trade and it was a side of Thailand that usually made Carl very angry. These girls would be totally under the control of some old hag and never dare to question her power. It was a far cry from the go-go bars where the girls were relatively free agents. This was the ugly side of the Thai sex industry. He couldn't afford to be angry in his predicament so he just smiled and said, "Another night would be better, thank you. We must sleep tonight as we have things to do in the morning."

The man got up to leave. Then halfway to the door he stopped, turned around, and walked back and sat back down on the bed. "Do you want some boys? Nice young boys," he said as he studied Carl and George closely.

"No thank you," Carl told him pointing at George. "You see we have each other."

The man looked at George and looked back at Carl. He had not thought they were a gay couple. He had just been doing his job when he offered them the boys. He shrugged his shoulders in acceptance that he could not expect everybody's sexual preferences to be transparent to him even after all the years he had been opening and closing bedroom doors for them. Nothing surprised him anymore. Not in his line of work. He walked out of the room and closed and locked the door behind him.

George checked the door was thoroughly locked, then turned and said, "Phew, that was a close one." Which got Carl laughing, followed by him coughing up raw whisky that his laughter had made him swallow the wrong way. George started laughing as well and they both laughed like they had never laughed before until tears streamed down their faces. The man had unknowingly released the dense fog of tension that had been filling the room prior to his arrival. It felt good to laugh out loud. They felt alive.

They drank most of the whisky then slept, drunk, with their clothes on under the mirrored ceiling.

CHAPTER 18

Mad Mike was a journalist from the old school and an alcoholic in the grand colonial style, a relic living in a postcolonial world. His pugilist's nose was crooked, big and red. A colour that matched the sweat-drenched thinning red hair that was permanently stuck to the top of his head and the ruddy face that was a canvas for broken blood vessels. All in all his fair skin and sweat-producing large build were not designed for tropical living. The most unlikely expatriates were always the most committed.

He had few friends because he was a bloody nightmare to be out in public with. His favourite stunt was to pick on the largest and most unpleasant looking man in the bar and say directly to him, 'See yoo Jimmy, Yoor urr hoomoosexual aren't yoo? Wee noo, wee noo. Its oolright you can coom oot noo. Yoo can coom oot of the closet noo, becoz wee noo.' There was always trouble when Mad Mike was around and drinking next to him was likely to make you collateral damage.

Once, briefly, he had been a regular at Oleg's bar on Soi Cowboy. Carl was there the day Oleg, bathing in the acceptance of such an expat icon, walked up to him and said, "I am so happy that you like my bar so much that you come here every day." Mike grunted and looked down at him from his slightly superior height and replied, "Can't stand the fucking place! It's just that I've been barred from every other gin joint on Cowboy."

Nobody knew how old he was so they just counted all the wars he had reported from. It was hard to tell from his damaged face what was a result of years and what was caused by booze and battles. He was old though; he had been around forever, or, as some people said, maybe it just seemed like it. At some point in his adult life he had worked for and been fired from every English language newspaper that Carl had ever read. His wildly improbable career meant he knew everybody in the newspaper game and that was why Carl was standing outside his house at 8 o'clock that morning.

The gate was open and the bell hadn't worked in years so Carl went in. It was an old duplex house with a small garden. It had been built in the 1960s and was typical of the lower cost houses that were rented to foreigners living on a tight budget. Its continued existence suggested that the patriarch or matriarch of the owning family was still alive as these houses were regularly demolished and the land sold after being inherited by the next generation. A little dilapidated but not an unpleasant place to live. Mad Mike had lived in the house for decades and paid very little rent.

Mad Mike sat perspiring in his usual place, a rattan peacock chair on the small veranda facing the garden. As usual he had a bottle of cold Singha beer in his hand.

"Well, well, Don Quixote, as I live and breathe." His Glaswegian accent was always mild when there was nobody else present. He didn't seem to mind Carl knowing that he had an education. To the rest of the world he liked to be perceived as coming from an underprivileged background in some shit-hole in one of the poorer areas of Scotland, which left him quite mad and undereducated. Carl knew that was not really the case at all. His modest lifestyle was a result of being disowned by a moneyed family as opposed to the lack of one.

"How is that mad wife of yours then?" Mike asked with a wicked grin.

"Someone else's mad wife now, I assume."

"Best thing really. Childhood decides you know. Can't keep trying to change people's destiny Quixote. People's problems belong to them. Stop fighting windmills that don't belong to you is the best thing. Debauch and drink and dance instead, it is the Asian way. Much better for you I assure you. Fancy a beer?"

"I can't dance but I could do with a coffee if there's one going."

Mike's maid was hovering inside the house just behind the mosquito door. She was called for and dispatched to bring Carl his morning coffee, much to his relief. Sex hotels aren't much use for anything else and he had missed his morning caffeine.

"This is unusually early for you. Not in any trouble are you? I haven't seen you looking stressed and out of bed so early since I bumped into you that morning in Beirut in 1983."

"That wasn't stress, that was a combination of alcohol and dysentery. Beirut was one hell of a month."

"That it was. I was pleased to see that your dysentery didn't interfere with your drinking. Do you remember that night in the bar with the Swedish girls just 'round the corner from the Commodore Hotel?"

"I am hardly going to forget. Still got the scars." Carl touched a small half-moon scar on his right cheek.

"Pissed off the wrong people that night didn't I?" Mike said laughing.

"Everyone you pissed off in Beirut was the wrong person."

"Great days Quixote, such wonderful days."

"All days are wonderful if you get away with it. We were lucky in Beirut."

"People like us are always lucky Carl. Haven't you worked that out yet?"

"Always lucky until the day you're not. That's how life works."

"I can't die and go to hell for a while yet Quixote; I've been barred again." He laughed out loud.

"Can I pick that mighty brain of yours?"

"Just don't tell anyone where you found it."

"Deal. I have been looking into a very convoluted case. There is a central character, nasty piece of work. Ex-CIA from Vietnam now a Thai citizen and associate of General Amnuay."

"Doesn't have a real estate company by chance, does he?"

"How the hell could you know that?" Carl asked him, shocked.

"I tried to write a story about him years ago." Mike sat back in his chair and said, "I was looking into a story of guns disappearing from military bases and ending up in Japan. They were written off the army's inventory after arson that was reported as electrical fires. A shipment of guns was seized en route to Japan. They prosecuted a few small fish but never touched the big boys. I went to this dreadful man's office, calls himself Somchai. Can you believe that? I asked him why he seemed to have relationships with all the parties involved from Thailand to Japan. He just laughed at me. But the next day Quixote, the next bloody day all hell broke loose. I was looked at through a microscope, by departments you wouldn't want to know that you are even in the country. Dangerous men, the sort of men you wouldn't have a drink with at the bar in a brothel. Then visits from Special Branch and Military Intelligence. I have tilted at a few windmills in my time Quixote, but you don't fight these guys, you just don't do it. You aren't are you?"

"You fancy the role of Sancho Panza?"

"Not bloody likely you lunatic!"

"Mike I need to tell you a story, but you need to keep your mouth shut. My survival may depend on it."

"You know I'm discreet but only in the really important things."

It was true. Mad Mike was totally discreet in the big things. That's why Carl was there. So he told him a story. He even made sure that most of it was true.

Mike listened attentively and when Carl was finished he sat in silent thought. Then he leant forward, sipped from his beer, and said, "Bugger of a situation you've got yourself in!"

"Brilliant! Mike, absolutely fucking brilliant! I risk life and limb travelling across town with military hit-men looking for me just to hear you speak the bleeding obvious."

Mad Mike laughed and began speaking in a serious tone. "No paper in Thailand will run it. I

217

may believe you but to the rest of the world it will sound like paranoid ranting from, if I may say it, a foreign private detective with something of a dubious reputation. The only time the press will run the story is if he is arrested, then it goes on the front page. But it doesn't sound to me like an arrest is in any way imminent or even likely. From what you're telling me there is not even going to be an investigation into him. The world press won't have any interest in your claims; they will automatically assume that you are talking nonsense. Why should they take you seriously when the police are showing no interest in this man? You're the one in hiding and that hardly makes your opinions credible. Should you raise your head above the parapet you won't make it through the night. Yours is not a funeral I would enjoy, Quixote."

"Is there a light at the end of the tunnel that isn't an oncoming train?"

"As an atheist I can't recommend prayer and as a friend I won't make promises I can't keep. You are fighting the patronage system, the Mafia and the corruption that they pretend doesn't exist. You are fighting ghosts. The only enemy you can actually see provides serious income for them so the system will circle the wagons and protect him at all costs. These people have their foot soldiers in the police, army, underworld, and politics. You, on the other hand, are just a farang that they probably think shouldn't be here in the first place. They make the rules and this is their country."

"I'm not getting a warm fuzzy feeling Mike."

"Well you wouldn't, would you?"

He left Carl alone with his thoughts and went into the house. He returned a couple of minutes later with a full bottle of beer in his hand and sat back in the rattan chair. After making himself comfortable he told Carl, "I never thought I would be suggesting this to you, I always figured you as part of the furniture. But it doesn't matter how long you've called this place home, you are and always will be a foreigner. No way round that. You need to leave Thailand and never look back. Just go! That's what you tell other foreigners who fall foul of the system here. Start taking your own advice. The system is Kafkaesque when it plots against you. Those are your own words Quixote. You know what you need to do, you are not here to seek advice, instead you are looking for an accomplice. The decision is too large for you to make on your own so you're trying to get someone else to make it for you. Well, I've done what you wanted Quixote, I've told you what you already know. Pack your bags and smuggle yourself across the border. I know you know how to do that. And never look back."

"I haven't made up my mind yet."

"Don't wait too bloody long is my advice."

"You are right as always."

"You look wrecked. There is a spare room

upstairs, go and get some sleep. Nobody knows you are here so you can sleep soundly. Beirut rules my friend; when the bombs are going off never pass up a quiet opportunity to get some quality kip."

"Thank you," Carl told him. "I think I might just do that."

Carl was between the chair and the door of the house when a thought occurred to him. He turned and asked Mike, "The one thing that is really bothering me, the thing that makes no sense is, why would General Amnuay be involved with this stuff? This is street stuff, he should be way above all that by now."

Mad Mike thought for a moment, then looked at Carl and said, "This is one of those things from history that is not really a secret but just isn't talked about much. There were thirty-eight thousand Thai soldiers serving in Vietnam under the Americans. They were called volunteers, whatever that means. If memory serves, Amnuay was a very young and very junior officer that was sent to Vietnam in the early 1970s. He came back to Thailand as a wealthy man, which is why he rose from junior officer to the dizzy heights he has achieved. Work on the assumption that he was working for the same people in Langley that your man did all those years ago. If they share a very nasty past there should be no surprise to find out their present activities are not squeaky clean either."

"Every time I turn around I find another player in this story that used to be with the CIA. Does that mighty brain of yours have knowledge of any active CIA players presently based in Bangkok that I could reach out to, should it become necessary?"

"Of course it bloody does," Mad Mike said smiling. "You could approach Bart Barrows and let him know that Inman is on his turf, if he doesn't know already which he probably does. That might cramp Inman's style and give him some sleepless nights."

"Bart Barrows is CIA?" Carl blurted out in shock.

"Of course he is, you silly man. Didn't you ever wonder why every bar where journalists drank in Beirut, sooner or later, you would end up bumping into the dreaded Bart Barrows? What did you think he was doing there, on holiday? Buying bomb-damaged carpets? He's hardly the type. He's your man, Quixote," Mad Mike said laughing. "Carl Engel, super sleuth, can't spot a Langley man even when he's standing right in front of him."

"You are a gentleman and a scholar."

"And not necessarily in that order, and like I said, don't tell anyone Quixote."

"No problem Mike," Carl said as he left him and entered the house. Mike was right; he was tired and hung over, as usual.

CHAPTER 19

Carl woke up in Mad Mike's house to the noises of Bangkok, urban birds, distant traffic, food vendors, and the chatter of maids. They were comforting sounds when you'd been around them as long as he had. Everything around him felt familiar. It reminded him of several houses that he'd lived in when he was young. He was smack bang in the middle of Bangkok expatriate life. He could have been anywhere and during any era from his past. It took him a while to remember where he was and what day it was. Reality soon kicked in and his mind went back into hyper-drive.

The room was old but clean and tidy. He had never thought of Mike as the sort of person to keep a comfortable home. There was a small bathroom door across from the bed. Carl needed a cold shower to get his mind sharp. He turned the water on after confirming that there were soap and towels he could use.

The walls and floors of the house were relatively thin and he heard the sound of Elgar's

Cello Concerto rising from the ground floor. He recognised it as an old recording with Jacqueline du Pre playing cello. Well, it stood to reason; what other recording could Mad Mike have owned? By the time Carl was showered and dressed, Jacqueline du Pre was attacking the second movement. Carl went downstairs. He was ready for coffee and cigarettes.

The music was louder than he had first thought. Maybe the walls were not as thin as he had assumed. Mike's maid was nowhere to be seen. Which was a shame, Carl had been counting on a cup of that coffee. He went through the front door and saw Mike was still sitting in his grandiose peacock chair on his little veranda. Or, to be more accurate, Carl saw his dead body upright in the rattan chair. Mad Mike's throat had been cut and the amount of blood on the floor under the white chair and the red stain that entirely covered the front of his white T-shirt left Carl in no doubt that Mad Mike was dead. A half-full bottle of beer was on the table in front of him and Carl could see it was still cold by the consistency of the condensation on the outside of the bottle.

He had most probably been killed during the first movement of Elgar's Cello Concerto, while Carl was upstairs in the shower. Immediately Carl became too focused on self-preservation to mourn for his old friend. He could worry about that sort of thing later. The first priority should be to make sure they didn't get him too. Carl was still breathing, unlike Mike, so Carl's own safety was all that he should focus on. Like Mike said, it was time for Beirut rules and Beirut rules said you were to forget the dead and look after the living. The assassins would have gone already, Carl decided hopefully. It would not make sense for them to risk getting caught anywhere near the corpse so they would have had to be long gone. He touched his gun for reassurance.

Carl saw Mike's maid in the bushes with her neck broken as he hurriedly left the house by the front gate and walked without showing unnecessary speed along the small lane and away from the house. Having balanced the odds between the risk of accidentally bumping into the assassins, or staying at the house and risking the police catching him there with two dead bodies and an unlicensed gun, Carl had decided to leave as quickly as possible. His mind was running too fast and incoherently for him to pay it any attention so he focused solely on getting away as he walked toward the main road.

Carl found an empty taxi and jumped in. He told the taxi driver to take him to Central Department Store at Chidlom Road. He would switch taxis there just in case the taxi was local and would later be asked by the police about fares he had picked up on the day of the murder. Carl was going to impose on the Dutchman and he had no intention of drawing a straight line between Mike's house and the Dutchman's.

Once in the taxi he tried to get a grip on his confused thoughts. Did it happen because he was there, talking to Mike? Carl decided no. If they knew he was asleep upstairs then he would be dead too. Could anybody have known Carl was going to meet Mike today? Once again, the answer was no. Nobody in Bangkok even knew they were friends. Being a friend of Mad Mike's was guilt by association. His bad behaviour in public was because he didn't approve of people getting too close. Carl played along and kept his distance. So why did they kill Mike? Carl's only conclusion was that Inman knew that he had been on the journalist's radar in the past and had decided to remove all loose ends from his present. Inman may have assumed that sooner or later Carl would have compared notes with Mad Mike and that had most certainly put Mike at the top of his hit list.

Fuck! They had come over the wall and slit his throat while Carl was in the shower. Mad Mike would have been too drunk by that time of day to see them coming. There were probably two of them. They would have held Mike still while they used the knife. That's why he was still in the chair and sitting upright. Two men on the ground. That sounded like the team that tailed Carl from the airport. He felt a cold shiver run rapidly up his back.

Carl could hear Ben Webster's tenor saxophone as he got out of the fourth taxi that he had used to get to the Dutchman's house. Carl had expanded on his crooked line theory and had taken the scenic route from Central. The jazz music coming from the house told him that the Dutchman was at home.

Pim opened the gate for him, muttering to herself as usual. Her grumbling was going in one ear and out the other and Carl hadn't registered a word of it. He tried to smile at her but by her reaction it couldn't have been a nice smile. What did she expect? He was in shock for fuck's sake.

Carl removed his shoes and entered through the back door, the friend's entrance. He could smell the sickly sweet aroma of Nepali hashish smoke. The Dutchman was sitting on the sofa obviously stoned. It made no difference that he was high. The Dutchman was permanently stoned and it seemed to have very little effect on his ability to function.

"You're back?" the Dutchman said as Carl turned the volume down on the amplifier and went and sat beside him on the sofa.

Carl spoke as calmly as he could, "I am in serious trouble Dutchman. If anybody finds out that I am here your life will be in danger. Is it all right if I stay?"

"My house is your house Carl. Do you remember that cute French girl you met in a discotheque and brought back here late one night because you had promised her a joint? Back when you were the young playboy? You got stoned and screwed her in that closet."

"I don't think you understood me."

"I heard you. My point was that my house has always been your house."

"Thank you," Carl said. "I need a safe place to get my breath back."

"Should you tell me about it?"

"Better give me a while to get my head together. Then I'll tell you what I can."

"If that's what you want. You don't have to tell me."

"That's what I want. A moment."

"Pim! Carl needs a whisky. He is white as a ghost," he bellowed.

Carl gratefully drank the neat whisky in silence. His brain was still not functioning properly. He needed to give it a little time and a little more alcohol. Carl wanted to call George on his new safe phone. The trouble was he couldn't remember if it was actually safe. Carl drank some more whisky and tried to think it through. Yes, it was safe. He took the phone from his pocket and made the call.

"It's me," he told George. "Mad Mike's dead and it wasn't a heart attack. Do you know the Dutchman's house? I am holed up here until I work out what to do next."

"I'm on my way," he said and hung up.

"Mad Mike is dead?" the Dutchman asked.

Carl nodded. "He's gone."

"Oh, my God!" the Dutchman yelled. "He was the funniest man I ever met. A dreadful drunk but a brilliantly intelligent and entertaining man."

It wasn't much of a secret after all, Carl thought to himself. He immediately looked for something to divert his attention away from the mourning process. He could do all that later. Carl walked over to the sideboard and poured himself another shot of whisky and lit a cigarette. It was what Mike would have expected him to do.

"George will be here in a couple of hours," Carl told The Dutchman.

"Where the hell is he coming from? Pattaya?"

"No, Dutchman, he is close by, but he'll take the long way here."

"Jacqueline stopped by late last night, after Brown Sugar closed. She said she was worried about you and thought you were in trouble. She said you had that look about you. When I asked her what look she meant, she said, your scared look. She really knows you Carl, I've known you forever and I have never seen you look scared."

"Everybody gets scared, it's the price for being alive, she told me once. Jacqueline was always right about most things." She knew Carl far too well for his liking. He didn't let people get too close. Maybe that was the root of their problem, he thought.

George arrived slightly less than two hours

later. He brought news from the old man.

"Carl, the old man says he lost the target. He gave them the slip by jumping on a long-tail boat at the Oriental Pier. He had dinner at the Oriental Hotel and then came out of the hotel around 10 p.m. He went next door to the public pier and took the only boat there at that time. They watched him go upriver but had no way of following him. He hasn't gone home and he has not been to his office."

"So he gave the order to hit Mike and then disappeared the night before it was due to happen," Carl said.

"You don't think he was there, do you? Shook off the surveillance so he could be there for the kill," George asked Carl.

"He is certainly evil enough and sadistic enough so it would certainly be a possibility."

"Shit!" George said.

'Shit' was right. Inman may have been in the garden watching his men murdering Mike while Carl was upstairs in the shower. If that was the case he had missed his chance to win the war. Carl decided he would make sure Inman lived to regret that oversight.

The thought that he probably planned to be there to watch him die as well, the same way he had probably watched Mike die, somehow made Carl feel worse about the danger he was in. Imagining somebody killing him for money was one thing.

Picturing somebody getting extreme pleasure or sexual gratification from watching him die made him feel like throwing up. Carl's world had lost its charm and all he felt was darkness.

The Dutchman looked up at them from his sofa and said, "I have heard enough to know how much trouble you are in. Hide out here until you have a way back to safety. But do try to avoid getting me killed if you can. I like my life." The Dutchman's face was happy and serene. Not because he liked the situation but because he was stoned out of his skull. He looked down and started to roll another joint.

George looked at Carl and asked, "So what're you planning to do?"

"I'm planning to get angry."

"It's about time."

CHAPTER 20

Three heavyset men with New York accents sat in a stolen car watching the offices of Las Vegas Real Estate on Silom Road. They hadn't shaved, showered, or checked into a hotel, and all three of them were bad tempered and tired. The floor of the car had the debris of breakfast cheeseburgers and coffee. The air inside the car reeked of cigarettes, BO and fried food. They had arrived in Bangkok early that morning and making their flight had been a last-minute rush after receiving emergency instructions by long distance phone call. There was a recent photograph of Anthony Inman taped to the dashboard under the air conditioner.

An old man matching their photograph came out of the Las Vegas office building and walked with characteristic short quick steps along the pavement of Silom Road towards New Road where he was planning to have lunch followed by a cigar beside the river at the Oriental Hotel, as was his daily habit. He was in a fairly good mood; his stupid ex-partner was dead and the unexpected joker Carl Engel would also be as soon as he showed his face. The Cat and the Rat had dispatched Victor Boyle and Mad Mike with excellent efficiency and he looked forward to when they would catch up with his final annoyance.

The meddling private detective had proved to be a bigger problem than anticipated so he wanted him dealt with sooner rather than later. The sooner the better as he had recently ceased web communication with a wonderful prospect with round breasts and milky skin. Voluntarily letting his prey escape was not something he enjoyed doing but there were times when being prudent outranked all other requirements.

The thought of the man that had caused his recent setbacks altered his mood; Victor had always been a loser. In Vietnam he had become a hanger-on who did what he was told but always got overly excited by the blood and the screams of the victims, which was an embarrassment. He was such a weakling that he didn't know how to find girls on his own so had followed Inman around like a starving puppy waiting for him to drop him some leftover meat. When Inman had become totally bored with him and left Nevada with all of their money he hadn't expected Victor to be able to find him though he knew he would try. How had they found him? They never could before. Yes, watching Carl Engel die was going to bring him great pleasure.

Two men got out of the car and walked briskly along Silom Road until they caught up with their quarry. As the third man drove the car slowly along the road beside them they zapped the slick-haired old man with a stun gun that they had purchased from a street vendor's stall on lower Silom that morning. They had been pleasantly surprised to find that a full array of weapons was openly available for purchase from the street vendors in the tourist area of Bangkok. One of the men opened the back door of the car and the other man bundled the body onto the back seat. It was over in a moment and none of the local people showed any interest in the car or the foreigners as they sped away.

The old man regained consciousness in a room without daylight. He had been injected with something to put him to sleep in the car. Then later he'd been injected with something to wake him up. His mouth was dry and his head was frustratingly fuzzy. He was tied to a chair and saw there were three men in masks standing in front of him. The masks were the rubber Halloween kind that can be found in the toy sections of department stores. As the fuzziness in his head began to clear Anthony Inman realised he was completely immobile and naked. The man with the grey hair, he assumed the oldest of the three, leant forward and said, "You shouldn't have killed the fat man. He promised us a lot of money."

Anthony Inman looked at the grey-haired man and said nothing. The masked man with the fully grey head of shoulder-length hair pulled a chair across the floor from the other side of the room and sat down facing the prisoner. The naked Inman was shaking, this couldn't happen, he was the one with godly power and being made powerless was not a possibility that he had ever considered.

"You are Anthony Inman?"

Anthony Inman did not reply. He had been trained for such situations and was supposed to gather information and not provide it. His training had not prepared for him for how scared he was feeling though. He decided he must outsmart his captors. That was it, he told himself not to forget that he was the most intelligent being in the room. Even gods were tested from time to time.

The ghoul with the 1970s haircut sighed and sat back in the chair. He stared coldly at his captive with steely dark eyes. Then he leant forward again and put the coldest eyes Inman had ever seen close to his face and said, "This is only about the money. If the fat man lied and there's no money I'm going to be very pissed off. You won't like it if I get angry."

He sat back again and stroked his chin in contemplation. The grey-haired ghoul then took his fingers from his chin and clicked them above his head. The other two in their gory masks carried over a table, camping gas, a frying pan, a small bottle of olive oil and a clove of garlic. After the table was set up the grey-haired ghoul took a Swiss army knife from his pocket and opened it showing the small blade.

"Here is the way it's going to be. You get to keep your property and your stock investments. We get the loose cash in your bank accounts. Fail to communicate immediately and I'll remove one testicle and fry it with garlic and then I'll force you to eat it while it's still hot. The fat man told me you like watching girls eat their own genitals so don't think this is an idle threat. Then I'll do the same with the other testicle. Once you have become a eunuch I'll give you ten minutes before I cut your throat. Your only way out of here and back to your life is to make a fast deal. I've no patience for psychological torture techniques so you need to understand that this is a straightforward ultimatum. As you know, an ultimatum is pointless without the will to carry it out. It would be foolish to doubt my will. Now I'm going outside to smoke a cigarette. When I come back you can make a deal with me or you're eating your testicle fried in garlic."

The grey-haired ghoul took a cigarette from his shirt pocket and left the room. Inman sat naked in the chair shaking and sweating as the two remaining masked men stood calmly in the corner of the room watching him. His mind was racing and he had no idea what he was supposed to do. He had been trained in counter interrogation and torture techniques but he had no idea how to deal with such a shocking ultimatum from a grey-haired ghoul.

He heard the door open and close behind him, telling him that the grey-haired ghoul was back in the room. The man slowly and deliberately turned on the camping gas and lit it with a disposable lighter. He poured a little olive oil into the frying pan and put it on the heat. With the blade of the Swiss army knife he opened and sliced a clove of garlic, which he put in the bubbling hot oil, filling the room with the pungent cooking smell.

"No salt and pepper?" he barked at his accomplices. "He should have salt and pepper on it."

The grey-haired ghoul then sat in his chair, leaned forward, and took the naked man's testicles in his left hand, and with his right hand he held the small penknife to the side of the sack.

"You have ten-seconds starting from now. Ten, nine, eight, seven, six, five, four, three, two."

Anthony Inman felt the small blade pressing into his scrotum. "What do you want me to do?" he yelled.

The grey-haired ghoul withdrew his hands and the knife and stood up and turned off the gas. He took another cigarette from his pocket and left the room without speaking another word.

A short man with dark hair and younger eyes sat in the chair in front of Inman. His face was hidden behind the rubber mask but Inman could see by his eyes that he was smiling.

"You wanna stay out of the frying pan you cooperate and you better hold nothing back," he said with the twang of street New York. "I'm an expert on bank accounts and internet banking processes. Our leader who you just saw leave the room is never going to speak to you again, never another motherfuckin' word. If he comes back it'll be to use the knife and the frying pan so don't try and lie to me. You will tell me about your accounts and the passwords and the security devices attached to those accounts. I will let you speak on a mobile phone to instruct a household member or a member of your office staff to retrieve the security devices and deliver them to a place of my choosing. Do you fully understand me?"

"I understand," Anthony Inman said shakily looking down at his intact genitalia.

Approximately ten hours later Anthony Inman woke up, fully dressed on the back seat of a car parked on the side of the road not far from Bangkok's airport. His head was full of cotton wool and his memory patchy as a result of the drugs that had been used to force him in and out of consciousness. His pockets were empty but there was a five hundred baht note sticking out of his shirt pocket. At least he had taxi money to get him home. He was a very angry and unhappy man and he felt weak and foolish. It had been an expensive afternoon.

CHAPTER 21

While Anthony Inman had been suffering his worst ever afternoon, his nemesis was only a few kilometres away having a quiet drink. Carl had spent a few hours in Candy's bar being prodded and pulled in all directions by the scantily dressed girls. He felt exposed being back there but was comforted by the knowledge that George was out on the street watching all of the comings and goings on Suriwongse Road. Candy's was busier than on his previous visit. Several barstools were occupied by early evening drinkers who had come straight from their nearby offices for fun and games before dinner, the usual crowd.

Carl finished his drink and walked to the toilet at the back of the bar. Mick Flynn grabbed him roughly as he went through the door. Mick was an extremely heavily muscled Irish building contractor with a drinking problem and permanent nosebleeds from the buckets of cocaine that he shoved up his nostrils all day and every day. He was dabbing at his nose with a blood stained handkerchief with his left hand as he grabbed Carl's arm in a death-grip with his right hand. His breath stank of Irish whisky and there were minute particles of white powder above his top lip.

"What the fook are you doin' here? I haven't seen you in ages," Mick shouted at Carl. His grip on Carl's arm was too fierce for Carl's liking. After snorting cocaine Mick had no idea of his strength.

"Just stopped off on my way home for a quick drink," Carl told him as he used his right hand to weaken Mick's grip on his left bicep.

"Dere's people bin asking after you on Patpong. It's not narcs is it?" Mick asked staring wildly. "They looked like feckin' narcs."

"Why would narcs be after me Mick?" Carl asked calmly.

"Because you're a friend of mine, you eejit. They nailed me last month and I had to pay them three-hundred-thousand to let me go. You know what they're like. They've probably already done the money and have come back for some more."

"I'm sure they weren't narcs Mick, so you can calm down and let go of me. I got caught screwing some rich banker's wife and he has set the dogs on me. So they're definitely not narcs Mick, and it's me they're after so you can let go of my fucking arm now."

Mick looked around the bar and then, still standing half in and half out the door to the toilet, he said, "Orright then. Do you want a couple of lines?"

"No thanks Mick. I have all the paranoia I need at the moment thank you."

"Please yourself," he said and let the door go behind him as he walked happily back into the bar.

Carl caught the door and went in to use the toilet. When he finished at the urinal he went to the cracked sink and splashed cold water on his face. He stood up with water dripping off his face onto his shirt. He looked at his tired unshaven reflection in the mirror and said, "Either you are totally mad or every other fucker in Bangkok is." Then he opened the door and walked back into the forever twilight of Candy's bar.

Bart Barrows had come in while Carl had been in the toilet and was sitting on his own in the middle of the bar waiting for his beer to be delivered. He was studying the activities and availability of Candy's girls like a hungry wolf. Carl moved up quietly and sat on the barstool beside him.

"Good evening Bart."

Bart Barrows turned and saw Carl. "Back again so soon? Have you given up your high society friends and come back down to earth at last?"

"Not really Bart, I'm here because I've been looking for you."

"Why would you be looking for me Carl? You spend most of your time avoiding me."

"It's about the people from your American

office."

"I don't have an office, I'm retired, but you know that." Bart was not talking like a buffoon for a change, which Carl found interesting.

"Yes you do. The huge one in Langley."

"What kind of mushrooms have you been sprinkling on your fried rice?"

"I know you're with the CIA Bart because a dead man told me. He knew all about you since Beirut. He was always smarter than me. I need your help for a change so the least you can do is listen," Carl said firmly.

"Go on then." Bart had stopped denying it at least, which was a better start than Carl had anticipated.

"I may be able to help you with some information. Anthony Inman is living in Bangkok under a Thai name and passport. He's a criminal and a serial killer and I know where he is."

"We know where he is Carl. His office is less than a mile from here," Bart said unusually sympathetically.

"Why on earth wouldn't you do something about it? He kills little girls and runs fucking guns to the Yakuza and god know what else."

"We know about the guns but you are full of shit if you think he's the serial killer, you would've been given that line of bullshit by Victor Boyle. He was always a liar. Surprised you bought it though. A little farfetched even for your infamous

242

imagination," Bart said gently.

"So if you know about the gun running how on earth is he still out walking the streets Bart?"

"Because as much as we despise Tony Inman, we've grown immeasurably fond of his associate General Amnuay and want him to be our best friend. He could be the next Chief of the Army, or don't you read the papers?"

Carl thought for a while and then said, "Bart, confidentiality is my business and you know I can keep my mouth shut if I choose to. It comes with a price though."

"It always does. And oh how painful is all payment." Bart was paraphrasing Lord Byron and Carl was staring at him open mouthed. Bart and Byron was a combination that beggared belief.

"You are going to write your mobile number on a piece of paper for me and one day soon I will call you and you will answer no matter where you are or what you are doing. That is all I ask in exchange for never telling a living soul that you are CIA. Fuck me around and I'll start putting deposits on advertising space. The mood I'm in at the moment I strongly recommend that you believe me." Carl's face had gone pale and his lips had become thinner.

Bart took a pen out of his shirt pocket and wrote his phone number on the back of a beer mat, which he handed to Carl. Bart looked at him in the eyes and said, "You are all right Carl, that is our opinion of you in the Bangkok office. Some of us have known you since you were a kid. But Carl, it's time for you to leave Thailand. These guys are out of your league and you are going to get yourself killed if you stay here."

"Doesn't sound to me like the CIA gives a fuck about civilians getting murdered. You know something Bart? They fucking well should."

"I just obey orders."

"I heard that excuse somewhere else. Just one more thing before I go. How is it possible that Art doesn't know Inman is here?" Carl asked as he folded the beer mat and put it in the back pocket of his jeans.

"Art would have done something stupid, killed him or at least told his friends at the FBI. Inman had some of Art's friends in Saigon killed and so Art wouldn't have played along with us. We had him working on the Cambodia desk for his last ten years and kept local operations from him. He was always drunk by eleven o'clock in the morning so it wasn't hard. Carl, you have promised me you can keep a secret. I don't want you letting me down on this."

"Take my call and I promise never to tell a living soul. I'll take it to my grave. And Bart, in spite of popular belief, I assure you that I plan to live to a ripe old age."

"I hope you do Carl. I really hope you do. We're all rooting for you." Bart turned his back to

Carl to collect his bottle of beer.

George came through the door with a crash and flew down the bar towards them. "They're here Carl, quick, is there a back way out of here?" he yelled as he slid to a stop in the middle of the bar.

Carl turned and moved quickly to the door into the toilet area. "I know a way out," he told George who was right behind him already.

They crashed through the door to the toilet and found Mick Flynn in front of the mirror wetting his handkerchief with cold water and holding it up to his nose again.

Carl stopped dead as George ran into him pressing him against the wall. Carl turned, his face pushed uncomfortably against the cold rough cement, and shouted to Mick, "Narcs Mick, two of them, right behind us. Block this door and dump the coke before they can get in." Then he grabbed George's arm and said, "This way!" He pointed at the staircase that was to the right of the toilet area. He ran up the stairs to the second floor with George close behind. As Carl turned the stairs he looked down and saw Mick's large frame pushing against the door as hard as he could. Staring at Carl he was yelling, "Yoo loyed, you knew dey was narcs. Oy can't believe you loyed to me."

At the rear of the building's second floor, in a room with women's clothing strewn over the bare concrete floor, was a large window that looked down on the grounds of a busy Buddhist temple. Carl picked up the solitary wooden chair and threw it through the window. "Now George!" They both took a running leap through the window, and after flying three meters through the air with their arms and legs going in all directions they fell a few feet and landed with a crash that put a serious dent in the tin roof of a hut that was part of the temple annex.

Their landing area was the temple's toilet and shower. The massive percussion noises made by the two big men crashing onto the thin tin roof received fearful screams from inside where a novice monk had been squatting on a toilet. He was new to the spiritual atmosphere of his new environment and although his mind was readily open to all things he hadn't anticipated the world exploding above his head, that had never been discussed, and so he had been taken totally by surprise.

They leapt down from the bent roof and into the temple grounds where they ran for the main entrance on the far side with Carl strongly outpaced by George but keeping up as best he could. The throngs of local people holding garlands and candles on their way into the sanctuary of the temple moved aside just in time as the two giant men came charging and yelling through their centre disrupting the calm joss stick infused air.

Once out on a street and well around the corner from Candy's bar, Carl and George headed toward Silom and kept running for a good ten minutes. At this point they decided it was safe to flag a taxi. They climbed in the back of the car wheezing and coughing much to the amusement of the driver. Carl told him that an angry bar girl was chasing them and if he wanted a tip he should put his foot down.

George's stolen car was not parked anywhere near Candy's. They had put it in the car park of an office building around the corner from Patpong and walked the remaining distance to the bar. As safe as they assumed it probably was they decided it best to wait a couple of hours before collecting it or possibly not to bother. Carl needed a drink, as usual.

CHAPTER 22

It was around midnight and Carl was lying on the back seat of yet another stolen car as George drove him to the nightclub. When they arrived he sat up and looked around. Everything out on the street looked relatively normal. The queue of people leading up to the security area with its airport style metal detector and front desk was typical of that time of night. Carl got out of the car and walked under the building through the parked cars. He entered via the back door and through the kitchen. George stayed outside in the car.

The colonel was standing in his usual place at the bar surrounded by the usual suspects. By the time Carl had crossed the crowded floor the bar staff had a drink prepared and on the bar waiting for him. Colonel Pornchai hadn't seen him come in so Carl tapped him on the shoulder. He saw Carl then took a quick glance around the busy nightclub to check for danger.

"You're living dangerously," he shouted above

the music. "I didn't expect to see you here."

Carl leant forward and said in his ear, "I'm being as careful as I can. We should talk in the kitchen."

They both picked up their drinks and walked to the kitchen, dodging the party people on the dance floor as they went. The kitchen had stopped serving food and the chefs and their helpers had gone home. Only the most junior of the kitchen staff were still there working and they cleaned up around Carl and the colonel. Carl put his drink down on a chopping board and turned to face him.

"I need something done," Carl said to him.

"Does it involve you staying out of trouble?"

"Yes it does, after this I'll be staying out of trouble," Carl told him.

"All right, go on then."

"There is a building on New Phetchburi Road." Carl handed him a piece of paper with the address written on it. "I need you to get a couple of boys from the drug squad to go and talk to the neighbours. They must make lots of noise and ask lots of questions about that building, and I mean a lot of noise."

"Is that all?"

"No. Then I want them to go to the local court and apply for a search warrant on the grounds that they have an informant that has told them the building is being used by youth gangs to store drugs and to host drug taking parties.

However, and this is the important part, they must make a mess of the search warrant application. I need the application rejected and submitted continuously for not less than two full working days. They must also be very rude and angry so that they argue with everybody working in the office at the court. Everybody in that department must become aware of this application."

"Are you sure this is necessary?"

"Totally necessary, and I need it done exactly the way I have asked."

"Why the drug squad?"

"Even the big shots will not interfere and tell the drug squad to back off," Carl told him. "Too much risk for them, by interfering they will go on the radar as possibly being involved in the drug business themselves. Under the present political climate that attention is something they will not want."

The colonel thought for a while and said, "The cost will be at least sixty-thousand baht."

"A hundred-thousand will be transferred to your account."

"Are you sure you know what you're doing?" he asked, obviously happy with the amount he was being paid.

"I hope so."

"Do you know that your friend Mike was murdered?"

"Yes. I was taking a shower upstairs in his

spare bedroom when they killed him."

"Maybe you should leave Thailand for a while."

"So people keep telling me."

"Don't go getting yourself killed just for the sake of being stubborn. I'll miss our business deals if you leave, but I don't make anything from you if you are dead."

"I am not planning to die."

"You won't have a choice. If they want you dead you'll die. You are a farang and they are Thai."

"Nobody will ever let me forget I am a farang. That is what I have going for me right now and why they won't see me coming."

"You are talking nonsense. Are you drunk?"

"Not yet."

Colonel Pornchai went back to the bar and Carl went the other direction via the kitchen sinks and left by the back door. He saw the car immediately. It was as close to the exit as was possible. George had kept the lights off but left the engine running. Carl looked up and down the street to make sure there was nothing out of the ordinary. All appeared normal so he got in the car and lay down on the back seat.

George drove through Bangkok for half an hour and parked the car outside Boonchoo's house. Boonchoo was their taxi surveillance man. Boonchoo lived with his family in one of Bangkok's oldest housing estates. The houses were very old but they all had small gardens, which made them more pleasant than most of the cheaper housing that the outskirts of Bangkok offered.

They got out of the car and rang the bell on the gate. Boonchoo and his son opened the rusty gate and greeted the pair with big old-fashioned genuine Thai smiles. Carl was always uncomfortable about his height around the people from the provinces as they were even smaller than the Bangkok Thais. Carl and George were a foot taller than Boonchoo and felt clumsy. Boonchoo's home was old and built for people like him, not giants like Carl and George.

He took them both by their hands and led them into the garden where a stone table with stone benches on each side had been prepared for them under a flame tree. They squeezed their large legs under the stone table and sat with their knees pressed against stone and buttocks partly hanging off the back of the bench. It was not a problem as long as neither one of them moved.

"Welcome to my house."

"Thank you Khun Boonchoo. I'm sorry it is the middle of the night."

"For you and Khun George any time is a good time."

The table was covered in small plates of food. A bucket full of ice and bottles of beer had been placed at the centre of the table. They were an old-fashioned north-eastern Thai family and while the men sat in the garden eating and drinking the women and young girls ran backwards and forwards to the kitchen carrying buckets of ice and plates of food.

They were nice people and they all looked after each other. Out of everybody in Carl's circle, Boonchoo was probably the most content. Carl and George spent a pleasant hour talking, eating, and drinking beer with ice cubes in it. Carl almost felt normal for a while.

After the meal Carl took the old man to one side and explained what he needed him to do. Carl told him George would be overseeing everything and offered to pay him up to date and for the days ahead.

"I know you have troubles so you don't have to pay me. I will do whatever is needed."

"Thank you Khun Boonchoo I know I can always rely on you. Money's the least of my worries at the moment so please take it."

He took the money reluctantly. Carl had always known that, in Thailand, the people with the least were always the most generous. They had some more drinks, then they both thanked him and his family politely for their hospitality and left. It was two in the morning.

Once inside the car George asked, "I've arranged a safe house like you asked. Do you want to go there?"

"Is it peaceful?"

"Quiet as a guilty conscience."

"All right chauffeur, stop by the hotel to pick up my stuff then drive me home."

They picked up Carl's meagre possessions and drove north for almost an hour. Then George turned off the highway onto dirt roads that meandered beside canals and fruit orchards. He stopped the car at a big wooden gate with a seemingly endless hedge on one side. He jumped out of the car and opened the double gate. Carl followed him out of the car so he could close the gates after George took the car in.

The driveway was very long and had a hedge on the right and a green field full of trees on the left. Carl walked after the car taking in the country smell of the place. The driveway ended at an old Thai style teak house that could not be seen from the dirt road. Carl walked around in the moonlight. It was very large and surrounded by orchards and ponds. Carl could hear the sounds of birds and animals all around him.

"It is incredible, you really are a wizard George."

"It belongs to a very old Englishman. It was to be his dream retirement home. Unfortunately it took so many years to build that by the time it was finished he was too old and sick to live so far away from a modern hospital. He lives in a small apartment with a view of Bumrungrad Hospital now. His children rent this place out to Thai television for their latest ghost series. I told them I had a Hollywood production team on a location hunt and they gave me the place for a few days so I can show it. Do you want to see the special rates they created for our Hollywood production?"

"I assume they are double what Thai TV are paying."

"Triple actually. Nice to see you haven't lost your cynical grip on reality."

"Contact them tomorrow and tell them that the scout is very excited and can't wait for the director to get here next week. A week should do us."

"Already did. I called them this afternoon."

"Hiding out in a ghost house!" Carl laughed out loud. "Pure genius. Even the assassins in this country are scared of ghosts."

They opened up the house and turned on some lights. At the back of the upstairs sitting room was a door that opened onto a very large wooden deck that ran the length of the entire house. To the side of the deck was a wooden stairway that went down to a pond that occupied the entire back section of the land. It was home to various kinds of birds and plants. It was straight out of old Siam, all except for Carl's favourite inhabitants, a pair of imported white swans that glided around the surface of the water like luxury yachts. They were imports.

"This is absolutely fucking wonderful

George."

"You want to hear the best bit? A Canadian lived here for a while. He rented the whole place for forty-thousand baht a month. The Thais won't live here because on television it's full of ghosts and the foreigners don't like it because it's in the middle of nowhere."

"Let's have a drink George. But when this is all over I want to rent this place."

"I'll go find a bottle of whisky and a couple of glasses," George said as he went into the house.

There were mosquitos but for once Carl didn't mind. This house was where he wanted to be. George came back and they sat drinking under the deck and looking at the private world of the old house bathed in moonlight.

When they had become comfortably numb George asked Carl, "How come you never talk about my wife?"

"Would it help if I did?"

"No it wouldn't, in fact it would make it worse."

"That's why I don't talk about it."

"I figured that was the reason," George said and then didn't feel like talking any more.

They sat in silence watching the swans glide backwards and forwards across the pond surrounded by the dances of the fireflies. After a couple more drinks they stumbled off to find their beds.

CHAPTER 23

Carl was woken at dawn by a screeching sound outside his bedroom window. It was a shocking grating noise and it was being made by something very close, too close for his liking. Carl pulled on his jeans and went outside to see what was going on.

George was already awake and sitting on the deck drinking coffee after having taken a ten-kilometre run and a shower. Carl was dehydrated and miserable. His head hurt, even his eyes hurt. He'd always seen George as an alien creature. What kind of person slept only a few hours, and then ran a ridiculously long distance with a smile on his face? Not Carl, that was for sure.

At the end of the deck perched on the wooden rail within a few feet of the window to the room where Carl had been sleeping was an adult peacock. His fan of a tail was open in all its multicoloured glory and he was jumping up and down on the wooden rail in all the excitement of wanting his opinion heard.

"What the fuck is that?" Carl asked.

"It's a peacock."

"I know it's a fucking peacock George. What's it doing screaming abuse at me outside my bedroom window?"

"Sorry, I forgot to mention Pretty Boy Floyd over there. He was another pet of the Canadian that used to live here. He was abandoned to be fed and looked after by the gardener, like the rest of the wildlife."

"Maybe you can reason with him. Tell him that all of us foreigners may look alike but it wasn't me that abandoned him."

Pretty Boy Floyd turned around to face them and continued to scream at Carl.

"I need a coffee," Carl told George as he walked away and re-entered the house. Carl was getting very attached to the house. It would be a wonderful life, away from the madness of central Bangkok and it was a long way from his enemies.

Carl found a coffee maker and a bottle of cold water in the kitchen. He went upstairs and found a dock for an iPod on the second floor landing connected to two battered speakers. He retrieved the iPod from his bedroom and plugged it in before selecting some appropriate morning music. Good morning Sibelius and welcome to paradise.

The violin concerto suited his mood. He carried the coffee mug and bottle of water out onto the deck and sat contentedly in the morning sun. Carl didn't have anything to do with his day. He had put a plan in process and had allowed it to run with its own momentum. Now he had nothing to do but wait.

"Where's the gardener?" he asked George.

"I told them we had some famous people arriving from Hollywood that didn't want to be bothered by paparazzi so he has been given the week off."

"Good move."

"I know you like your privacy. I'll take the car and do some running around today."

"Give the old man a call late afternoon while you're out."

"I'll do some shopping as well," George said, and then he was gone.

Carl heard the car engine disappearing into the distance. He went into the house and got a piece of paper and a pen, which he brought out to the deck. Carl always thought more clearly when he wrote things down, so he wrote out his entire plan. He then made notes beside each section with all the things that could go wrong. It was not perfect but he was not unhappy with it. It was all he had. He read it through one more time and then went down the steps to the garden and burnt the paper.

Carl had been hiding and looking over his shoulder for several days so he decided to take advantage of his rural surroundings and go for a walk. The ability to open the gate and walk along the dirt road through the orchards and over the small canal bridges was magical. Being a foreigner and of a certain age meant the local people didn't see him as a threat so he could ramble through their lanes and fields. It was midday and the heat meant the local dogs barked and postured but didn't really have the heart for a fight. Mad dogs and Englishmen go out in the midday sun, Carl thought. Well somebody has to do it.

He noted that the house he was staying at was isolated and the nearest neighbour was some distance away. He had walked for five minutes before seeing another occupied house. There was another wooden palatial residence a couple of hundred meters along the dirt road but it was rundown and empty. Probably a wealthy person from Bangkok who had been bitten by the nostalgia bug but lost interest when confronted with the reality of lengthy traffic jams, country smells and violent mosquitos. Carl noted how isolated he was and smiled. His plan had just got bigger.

He returned to the house a couple of hours later drenched in sweat. The car was not there, so George was still out checking on things for him. Good old George. The rule was that no phones were to be switched on within fifty kilometres of the house so Carl was totally without communication. He took a shower and put his wet clothes back on. He was still travelling a bit too light for his liking. He went to sit in the sun to dry off but immediately started sweating again. Carl stripped down to his boxer shorts and went looking for books.

There was a small room with a desk and a table light, behind which was a bookshelf with a few dozen mildewed paperback books. The shelves had the usual collection of semi-pornographic Muzak read by millions. Fortunately there were also a couple of gems. He picked out Death in the Afternoon by Ernest Hemingway. An unfortunate title in his recent predicament, but it was a wonderful escape into the world of Spanish bullfighting. Carl threw himself into the nostalgia of a Spain from the past, sitting in his garden from old Siam. All in all he had a very pleasant afternoon.

George came back around five o'clock with plastic supermarket bags and a paper shopping bag containing new jeans and casual cotton shirts. Carl immediately took a cold shower and put on the new clothes. Carl felt good, surprisingly happy. He was in the Thailand he had fallen in love with in his youth. More accurately Carl had fallen in love with what Thailand could have been like for him. He had probably fallen in love with pictures of old Siam. Carl's life was a series of adventures falling in love with things that only existed in books, so that was probably the case. The house may have only been an oasis in the present day chaos that was modern Thailand but an oasis is big enough for one man. Carl dared to dream for a while.

George was suddenly all businesslike and he pulled Carl back to reality. Carl didn't like it.

"Boonchoo and his son were in the noodle shop behind the old office like you asked," George told him. "Some nasty looking cops showed up, plain clothes boys. They asked lots of questions all round the neighbourhood. Lots of questions about youth gangs and drug parties at that building."

"And?" Carl asked impatiently.

"After they left, the woman from the dress shop walked around asking everybody what'd been said. Then she went back to her shop and sat talking on her mobile phone for half an hour. What was that all about?"

"She's the gossip he left behind."

"I don't get you."

"Inman would always have maintained a relationship with the local gossip. A strong relationship with constant contact, presents at Christmas and children's birthdays. He has a secret in that building so he would monitor the events around it. We can assume he has now been told that the drug squad has an interest in the building."

"How do you know he would've done that?" George asked him.

"Because it's what I would have done."

"So what happens now?"

"Now George? Now we eat and drink

ourselves silly. I like it here and I intend to be very happy for as long as I can."

Carl entered the door that led from the deck to the second floor landing and selected a 1953 mono recording of the opera Tosca with Di Stefano and Callas singing their hearts out beautifully. The speakers' veneers had peeled in the humidity leaving them looking worthless but their sound was excellent.

He went to the kitchen to see what George had brought home in the plastic supermarket bags. There were all sorts of food items including a baguette, walnuts, dried figs, Gorgonzola cheese and spaghetti. He put all of the other items in the fridge. This was going to be very easy, and there were some bottles of Chilean red wine that looked very drinkable.

Carl boiled the pasta al dente and fried the walnuts with a little butter. He would have preferred to use walnut oil but his circumstances required a few small sacrifices. He tossed the spaghetti with the butter and walnuts. Then, as it cooled just slightly, he threw in chopped dried figs and Gorgonzola cheese, tossed the whole lot with some black pepper, and put it all in a serving bowl. He put a bottle of red wine under his arm, grabbed the baguette, plates and two wine glasses, and headed back upstairs. Dinner was served.

Later in the evening they opened a second bottle of wine and George said, "I have just realised something."

"Pray tell."

"The worse this situation becomes the more you seem to be enjoying yourself."

"Other people have said that about me in the past."

"How does that work?" George asked.

"Buggered if I know."

They watched the swans majestically manoeuvring around the pond and drank their wine in silence. Carl thought of the life that had brought him here. He thought about the women along the way. But mostly he thought about her. There's always one.

By eleven o'clock Carl was comfortably numb again. There was nobody within hearing distance so the music had got louder as the empty bottles had accumulated, ceremoniously laid down on the deck like dead soldiers.

When Tosca had thrown herself noisily from the parapet thereby ending the opera Carl decided to stick with Callas and Di Stefano and put on La Boheme. The bohemian opera was in its final act by the time the wine was getting difficult to swallow and felt like it was on the verge of coming out of Carl's ears.

"What is your fascination with Puccini operas?" George slurred.

Carl sat thinking, which was not easy given how drunk he was. "It's about the real things, the important things; life, love, relationships, loss, death. In real life there are no happy endings George. Happy endings are a con trick. The trick is convincing the audience that the story is over when it isn't. If you follow any story to its true conclusion it must end badly. All life may begin with a miracle but it must always end with a tragedy. That is the nature of life."

"You're a cheerful drinking companion tonight."

"Sorry George. Don't ask the question if you think you won't like the answer."

Pretty Boy Floyd could be expected to deliver his morning diatribe outside Carl's bedroom window again so an early night suddenly seemed like a very good idea. Carl stood up and went to the rail where he stood like a latter day Alexander surveying his kingdom. Having committed it to memory he slurred a goodnight to George and left the deck.

Carl went to bed dreaming nostalgic thoughts about spending his future playing a country squire in old Siam. Nostalgic thoughts do not live in a vacuum though so the idyllic country lane became memory lane. Thanks to the vast quantities of wine he had consumed he fell asleep anyway.

CHAPTER 24

The rising of the sun and arrival of the new day was screeched into Carl's bedroom by Pretty Boy Floyd. He was perched on the rail of the deck near the bedroom window again, angrily bouncing up and down from the knees with his plumage fully fanned out. Carl was getting rather fond of him and his funny habits.

Carl's head was fuzzy but he was not unhappy with the early alarm call. The fresh air was having a positive effect on his sense of well-being. It had rained during the night and the air was cool and fresh. Carl went for a walk through the grounds, barefoot on the wet grass. There was life everywhere he looked: small birds, large birds, squirrels, butterflies and bugs. It was good.

Carl returned to the house for an early breakfast with George. He went to the kitchen and made them both what he claimed was a nice health-conscious fry-up. In reality it was a good old-fashioned greasy spoon special. Even the bread was fried. He pointed proudly at a grilled tomato on George's plate amongst the bacon, sausages, greasy eggs, fried white bread and deep fried potatoes and said, "Vitamin C. That will sort you out."

After they had finished what was on their plates he asked George if he could check in with the old man sometime in the mid-afternoon, to make sure everybody was doing whatever they were supposed to be doing. There was no room for errors or delays. Everything had to be perfectly synchronised like a circle of white bathing capped Nazi frauleins in a swimming pool. George would supervise all of the teams and technicians personally, so he would be away until the following afternoon.

Carl was planning a lazy day hanging out at his temporary summer palace and doing as little as possible. That would make the day even better. As big as the house was Carl liked it best when it was just occupied by him and the birds. He was still very much a lone wolf.

Carl had two phone calls to make before he took the rest of the day off. The first was to his favourite journalist, Kenny Burns. He used to be Carl's second favourite but with Mad Mike's demise he had been promoted. Kenny Burns was from the school of the Cambodian Killing Fields and was totally fearless. Some of his friends had died in Cambodia back in the 1970s and he had survivor's guilt that manifested itself in blindly walking into danger as long as he felt it newsworthy. He had a partner, Heinz Fogel, a German cameraman with an extremely large newsman's camera that he had received in 1975 in payment for a debt from a Russian in Phnom Penn. It was the camera Carl wanted most. It would get plenty of attention.

Carl had not told George that he was planning to break their agreement of not switching any phones on at the house. There were things that George didn't need to know about. He had seen a couple of new SIM cards in the shopping bags in the kitchen the previous night and he had put them on top of the fridge. Now he went and got one. Having inserted it into his phone he made the call. Carl was beginning to be careless but he knew it wasn't going to be a problem. Things were moving fast enough now for Carl not to care about leaving some tracks behind him.

Carl had a very difficult job convincing Kenny that he should take his money to run the sham news story he was asking for. Journalist's ethics and all that. But he was a friend and he eventually agreed. All Carl was hoping was that someone would speak enough English to understand the show that Kenny and Heinz would be putting on.

The second phone call was to Bart Barrows.

"Bart, it's me," he said, not using his own name intentionally. Special Branch probably listened to every call Bart made.

"Yeah," Bart said.

"Bart, remember our deal. I want you to call that bloke and say this and only this, 'That motherfucker of a PI is making a stink and there's going to be trouble'."

"That's all you want?"

"That's it."

"Sounds like a pretty good horse trade to me."

"I will call you again tomorrow with details of a time and a place for a meeting. I have a solution that I think will work for everybody. After that I'll keep my promise."

"It's a good idea to be sensible and negotiate. Everything is a compromise in Thailand. I was worried you had forgotten," Bart said unusually intelligently. He would always have his CIA hat on for Carl from then on.

Carl disconnected and switched off the phone by removing the battery. Why was Bart so keen on a peaceful settlement? Perhaps turning a blind eye to the activities of a low life like Anthony Inman to keep the general happy was sticking in his craw. Could Bart be an ally?

At midday Kenny and Heinz arrived at the building on Phetchburi Road and set up the giant camera. Kenny stood with the building as a backdrop and spoke loudly into the microphone in his hand.

"In this ordinary building that you see behind me shocking events have been occurring. In the next few days, stories of CIA operatives, senior military officers, gun running, drug trafficking, and murder will be revealed. Remember the building behind me and remember who brought you the news first. This is Jack Kerouac reporting from Bangkok."

Later Kenny told Carl that people came out onto the street to see what was going on. Kenny, sweating profusely, complained about the light and sometimes complained about the sound as he repeated the report in front of his growing audience seven times. If anybody in the audience had looked closely they would have seen that the camera wasn't switched on and hadn't been for decades. After the seventh take Kenny and Heinz packed up the camera and left the scene of the crime.

By the late afternoon Carl had finished Death in the Afternoon and his hangover had retreated to a safe distance. He took a shower and listened to some Mozart. Carl did a few mental checks and took the gun out from under the mattress where he'd been keeping it. There were five bullets in it and he had no extra ammunition. Five bullets would have to be enough and he would have to live without target practice. It had been many years since Carl had held a pistol.

Carl didn't like guns. He never had. They are made for one purpose and worshipped by the sort of people that Carl didn't want as his neighbours. Getting older is a long series of compromises and he had experienced his fair share. Carl tucked the gun in the back of his jeans so it sat in the small of his back where a loose hanging shirt would easily hide it.

He went to the kitchen and made himself an omelette and a very large cup of coffee. He sat at a table beside the pond and under the shade of the deck. It was shelter from the sun and he felt closer to the animals down there. The swans looked at him suspiciously and the ducks moved to the other side of the pond. Carl's peaceful place as a child had been a duck pond on a local common in south London. He used to go there in all weathers to think. The wooden house made him feel like a child again. He was going to be sorry to leave it.

Carl had made his decision on the inevitable outcome of his case a couple of days earlier. It was dangerous to second guess himself after he had committed to a course of action, but Carl grew up in England and that was typically what English people did. Things were destined to run their course and whatever the outcome there was no going back. Instructions had been given and George would be arranging everybody's payments.

Anthony Inman had been CIA in Vietnam so there were most likely drugs somewhere in his past as well. He had made his fortune torturing people and then executing them if they couldn't afford to pay him and his cronies. He must have enjoyed it because he took it up as a hobby and then made it part of his sex life. He had been involved in various criminal activities since his arrival in Thailand. Gun running Carl was aware of and he could guess at the rest. Inman had become Carl's nemesis through serendipity and his own foolishness. Carl's enemy was the worst foreigner in Thailand. He had never done things by halves.

Carl retrieved his old Blackberry from the bedroom and took it out to the deck where he placed it on the table and lit a cigar. After an hour of pondering the pungent smoke and the communication device he stubbed out the cigar and turned the Blackberry on. He watched it booting and downloading messages and emails. Then having confirmed it was working properly he took it into the bedroom and put it on the bedside table.

Carl went book hunting again and selected Burmese Days by George Orwell. He went back to the bedroom and lay down on the bed, having taken the gun from the small of his back and placed it on the bedside table. After an hour of reading he realised how little South-east Asia had changed in the last hundred years. Orwell's world of drunken expatriates and venal bureaucrats rang lots of bells. He put the book on the side table and did something very uncharacteristic – he took a nap.

CHAPTER 25

The Cat and the Rat came after midnight pushing their motorcycle the last half-kilometre so as not to be heard. They hid the bike in the bushes not far from the large wooden gate and paused to take a smoky hit of speed burnt on tin foil. Since having to leave the army they had developed a taste for yah bah, crazy pills in English, and had both developed the sunken cheeks and vacant eyes of the habitual user. They checked their automatic pistols and military knives before climbing over the gate into the darkness.

They both landed quietly on the driveway, legs bent like springs as they had been taught by a stern sergeant major prior to being pushed out of an airplane during their military training. Having read the terrain they both went left into the orchard and hid amongst its trees while their eyes became acclimatised to the pitch black provided by the canopy of branches and leaves that kept out the light from the moon and the stars.

In the distance they were relieved to see lights

on at the house telling them that he was there. They slowly made their way through the orchard. When they got close to the house they saw there was an open lawn between them and the side of the house. This open area was well lit by the moon and the lights coming from the windows of the house.

"We must cross it," the Cat told the Rat.

"Together and quickly," the Rat whispered.

They both moved rapidly carrying the top half of their bodies low until they reached the teak house. They stood with their backs to the house listening for any telltale sound that would mean they had been seen crossing the open lawn. No sound came.

"Look how this farang lives, like a prince. I will enjoy killing him," the Rat whispered in the Cat's ear. The Cat smiled.

They made their way slowly around the house to the back where the pond was and slid along the wall under the deck to the back door, which they were pleased to find was open. The Cat looked through the crack at the side of the door and signalled that Carl wasn't downstairs. They entered the house with the stealth that had become their second nature. After checking there was nobody in the kitchen they slowly began to creep up the wooden stairs.

The second floor was well lit and there was a half-finished whisky bottle and an empty glass on a round table at the centre of the landing between the three bedroom doors. Only one of the bedrooms had lights on but they quietly checked the two dark bedrooms as they had been trained. Having confirmed they were empty they took up positions on each side of the occupied bedroom door.

They communicated by hand signals then opened the door and went in together, one high one low, with guns drawn as they had been taught. The room was empty. There was the Blackberry with its signal that had led them to the house and an open book lying face down on the bedside table and there were clothes strewn on the floor but no Carl. The Cat and the Rat sat on the bed, guns casually on their laps but pointed at the door, and evaluated their situation.

"Do you think he's in the garden?" the Cat asked the Rat.

"We would have seen or heard him."

"What do you think is going on?" the Cat asked.

"Who knows what these farangs do?"

"Let's get out of here and kill him on the street tomorrow when he goes out."

"Do we have enough stuff for a stakeout?"

"I have six pills."

"OK. Then we will kill him tomorrow in daylight. Maybe the ghosts are protecting him here and that is why we can't see him."

"That is probably it. Only a stupid farang would live in a haunted house."

Under their dark green military combat jackets and T-shirts they were both covered in the religious black ink tattoos that they believed protected them from all of the dangers of their chosen profession, the most important two of which were ghosts and bullets. The tattoos ran from their waists to their necks both front and back and had taken years of enduring pain from hand-tapped needles to complete. Their protective tattoos were the reason they had reluctantly agreed to enter the haunted house that had been made famous on television.

They slowly retraced their steps back down through the house and across the lawn to the orchard. They sat for a while and watched the house for any movement but there wasn't any so they made their way through the orchard and climbed back over the gate.

"Where're the pills?" the Rat asked. "I hate ghosts."

"In the bike. I'll get one for you."

The Cat went to the bushes where they had stashed the bike and Carl walked out from the dense foliage and shot him in the chest. Carl kept walking forward firing at the Rat. He knew he wasn't a great shot so he made sure he got closer every time he fired. He saw two out of three bullets hit him in the middle of his body and saw him drop like a stone. When he turned around he saw that the Cat was still alive, breathing bubbling red foam but trying to stand up. He walked back to where the Cat was trying to use the bike to pull himself up from the ground.

"Who are you? They said you were an ordinary person. How come you shot us?"

Carl put the gun to his head and said, "I'm very ordinary until people start killing my friends." Then he shot him with his last bullet, point blank, and saw the brains vomited out of the back of his head.

Carl had spent the late evening digging a hole in the far corner of the orchard by the beam from a torch. It was backbreaking work and he hurt all over from it. He opened the gate and dragged the bodies one at a time and dumped them in the hole. Then he went and got the torch that he had placed on the ground behind their motorcycle, where he had been waiting for them to give up the hunt and do what was inevitable and return to their means of transportation. He closed the gate and walked back to the corner of the orchard and buried them by torchlight. Two hours later he patted down the earth and carried the shovel back to the house. He needed a drink badly but for a change the drink he craved was water.

He sat under the deck watching the swans and the fireflies and drank a litre of cold water straight from the bottle. The gun was on the round marble table beside him and he picked it up and threw it in the pond, much to the disapproval of the two swans. He had no more bullets and so the pistol was of no further use to him. The colonel had said it was untraceable so it would make no difference if it was found one day and linked to the bodies in the grave in the corner of the orchard.

Carl was counting on the bodies not being found for a long time, putting distance between him and his brief stay at the house. George had used an alias so given time they would not link a Hollywood film crew to the time of the shooting of two known assassins and there would be no way of putting Carl or George in the area. They probably wouldn't try, as it would offend them to believe mere foreigners had killed such notorious assassins.

He closed up the house for the night and took a shower and went to bed. He was totally exhausted. He had had a very long day. As he was going to sleep he thought to himself that it was a good thing he was moving out the next day. It wasn't that he hadn't fallen in love with the place; he had. It was that it had suddenly occurred to him that if there weren't any ghosts before there sure as hell were now!

CHAPTER 26

It was already noon when Carl heard the car coming up the dirt driveway. He had slept seven hours and was still in bed. He had been so sound asleep that even Pretty Boy Floyd had been unable to wake him in spite of giving it his best vocal effort to date. Carl rallied his aching body and went out to the deck. The clear blue sky and bright sun alleviated some of his aches and pains. It looked like it was a very nice day.

A few minutes later George came and sat at the table. He seemed excited.

"What's up George?"

"Boonchoo went to the court building like you asked him to. This morning was his second day there. As you told him to expect, there were arguments over the application for a search warrant on the Phetchburi Road address. The drug squad boys were in and out of the court since yesterday afternoon. There were strange people sitting around since early this morning. They called someone on their phone and told them what was

279

happening. Boonchoo said they must've been talking to someone very important. Lots of grovelling was taking place from what he could hear."

"Good."

"What does it mean?" George asked.

"It means they'll be circling the wagons and so you have to tell the owner of the house that Hollywood is not interested at present. We are leaving today. I'm going to miss this place."

"Where are we going?"

"It's time to end this. Everything should be ready and there is work to be done. I assume everybody showed up and did what was asked?"

"They did."

"How were Damien's Finns?"

"Speaking techno babble in three languages as usual."

"You paid them well?"

"Just like you told me to. It may not have been necessary; they are still grateful for what you did for them with their visa problem at immigration."

"It is always important to pay people well."

"Maybe that's why you are always broke."

"And Damien doesn't know what they are doing?"

"Not as far as I know."

"Not that it would make much difference," Carl said. "Better for him if he doesn't know."

"They're professionals and have IQs through

280

the roof. They said they could meet your time requirements and I saw no reason to doubt them. They said to tell you not to worry, they won't let you down."

"That's good. Then we need to pack up and leave. We'll wipe the house down for fingerprints before we go."

"Is that necessary?" George asked.

"You can never be too careful," Carl told him and went to the bedroom to pack his belongings back into their shopping bags. He wasn't going to tell George about his revenge on the two assassins. The trick to getting away with murder is not telling anybody.

They left the house late that afternoon. Carl watched through the rear window of the car until he couldn't see the Thai roof any more. After a while the car left the rough laterite and they were driving on smoother asphalt. The car was making good time towards Bangkok. When they reached the early evening traffic on the outskirts of the city their progress slowed to a snail's pace. Carl wasn't worried about the gridlock. He knew that they had plenty of time.

He picked up his phone and called Bart Barrows.

"You need to get General Amnuay to Inman's old office on Phetchburi Road tonight at midnight. You can tell him that I'm ready to make a deal. If he doesn't show up tell him he will be able to find me at the Foreign Correspondents Club buying drinks for foreign journalists."

"What makes you so sure I can get him there?" Bart asked.

"He knows police and journalists are already sniffing around Inman and his safe house."

"So why will he meet you?"

"Because you all want me to go away Bart so of course you'll all come," Carl told him. Bart stayed silent so Carl hung up.

"Can I ask the question?" George requested.

"Go ahead," Carl told him.

"I know how it works Carl. You don't tell people your whole plan. I go along with that, but in the past I've always understood your process. This plan you are playing out worries me because it seems overly complex. So complicated that I have no idea what you are up to."

"That's because what you are watching is the absence of my standard type plan. I gave up days ago. There is no magical solution this time. I don't have jigsaw pieces juggled in the air ready to fall neatly into place. The system here is conveniently corrupt but this time it's working against me. I'm up against somebody that has been manipulating the system for longer than I have. He has the large amounts money and the connections to get away with murder, literally. His friends are now my enemies and they have all the power, it's their country and I'm nothing but a foreigner they choose to tolerate, at least for now, like all foreigners."

"So what does all that mean?" George asked.

"It means I am running a bluff and if they don't fold their cards I'm finished, game over. What I've done will eventually bring them down anyway but I won't be alive to see it. For me to win they must fold their cards."

"Why don't you want me there?"

"I need to surprise them. If you are there it will appear confrontational and if they choose violence over dialogue then the game is over."

"But what if they send the soldiers I saw following you at the airport?"

"They won't," Carl told him.

"I hope you know what you are doing."

Then Carl explained to George where they were going and why. He told him that they were dumping the car and leaving for the islands the following morning. Carl told him that they would reinvent themselves and the islands would make everything good for a while. He told George that his dead wife would want him to move on and give up his house full of memories where every corner he turned he still expected to bump into her. And Carl told him that, after what was going to happen that night it would be time to start living again. George had no more questions so they drove the rest of the way in silence.

CHAPTER 27

Through the heavy soundproof window Carl could see the cars on the road outside flashing past the building. It was late and the roads of Bangkok had sped up. A stream of headlights flowed in both directions either going to or coming from one of Bangkok's nocturnal pleasures. He wondered how many crimes were being committed that would never be discovered. Some of the drivers had to be transporting drugs, taking bets on their mobile phones, trafficking underage girls, or possibly even preparing to commit murder. The statistics said that some of the cars' occupants had to be breaking the law, drunk driving at least. Laws are about controlling society. Their purpose is not to make sense of it. Law enforcement became involved when, often by sheer accident, they were made aware of a crime and it was topical enough to deserve their resources. Unfortunately, in Thailand, even then it did not always get the desired result.

Inside, everything was ready and the musty

room had taken on the appearance of a well-organised classroom. George and Boonchoo's family had played their parts in the new décor and the Finns had come in late that afternoon to add the final touches. Carl stood alone by the window, waiting with the lights off.

Outside, Phetchburi Road was a sea of colour as the headlights fought with the neon signs for dominance. The light and shadow against the wall with its dreadful metal ring to restrain victims appeared like something straight out of an early black and white horror film. The hairs on the back of Carl's neck were standing up and his stomach was a bucket of eels. He thought about time and how it would pass with or without him wrestling with it. He made himself focus on the reality that what was in front of him would soon be something that was behind him, leaving all negative feelings, fear and pain redundant. 'God give me patience; but I want it right now!' he told himself.

The room he was waiting in had been witness to repeated performances of the ultimate crime, the killing of human beings for pleasure. Experts can rationalise the behaviour of such men but rationalising is not the same as understanding. Shakespeare wrote in his final play, 'Hell is empty and all the devils are here'. Such cynical conclusions often come at the tail end of a man's existence. Perhaps because he can look back without the fear that is always present when looking forward. The other possibility is that age just makes man negative and bad-tempered. Something we then confuse with wisdom. Carl didn't much care where his reasoning had come from. He had already made his choices and it was too late to turn back.

Carl smelled the petrol before he heard the footsteps. It wafted up the stairs like napalm on the night air. Then he heard the clink of glass bottles getting louder as Inman climbed higher. Anthony Inman entered the room that had once been his office and later had become his second floor dungeon of dirty tricks. He wore a polo shirt, cotton trousers, and an expensive-looking pair of brown leather moccasins. His hair was grey and perfectly groomed in the old slicked down Brylcreem style with a side parting. He was tanned and physically fit. He looked a hell of a lot better than Carl did. He placed the plastic supermarket bags containing glass bottles of petrol on the floor. He reached into his pocket for a large wad of cotton material and a lighter, which he put down beside them, the tools of the traditional arsonist.

He didn't see Carl at first. Carl stood quietly in the shadows and watched the most evil man he had ever had the misfortune to cross paths with wistfully surveying the dreadful room. Carl remained silent and still as Inman's body language changed as he began to sense that there had been unwanted visitors and changes had been made to his lair during his absence.

He switched on the light, turned around and saw Carl. Inman appeared more annoyed than concerned as he pulled out an expensive-looking pearl-handled Desert Eagle .357 Magnum automatic pistol and pointed it at the private detective. It made perfect sense to Carl. If a man's in the arms business you had to expect him to be carrying expensive equipment.

"What are you doing here you dumb motherfucker? Never mind, it'll be good that they find your body in the ashes."

"Be hard to stick the murders on me if I have bullets in me."

"You're right. Now turn around and put your hands behind your head."

"I'm not going to do that. You need to wait for Amnuay and Bart. Forgive the cowboy rhetoric but the building's surrounded."

"You're such an arrogant motherfucker. Don't you have any concept of how out of your depth you are?"

"Those noises you just heard from downstairs are General Amnuay and Bart. And by the sound of all those heavy feet the general has brought help."

"Good! I always appreciate some backup," Inman said with a confident razor-thin smile.

"So this is where you like to hurt people?" Carl asked him.

"Guess what motherfucker? You're next," Inman snarled.

"Now you have the Thai army and the CIA here to help you it should be a fairly even contest."

"Fuck you!" he said snarling again.

"Is that all you have to say? Consider some well-chosen last words. Time is not something you should be wasting. You don't have much of it left."

"I'm going to get great pleasure from killing you," Inman told him grinning like a Cheshire cat.

Carl had handled the situation and bought the time he needed. As long as Inman was talking he wasn't shooting. The herd of feet reached the entrance to the room and General Amnuay and Bart Barrows entered, leaving a squad of soldiers lining the stairwell. They both surveyed the room and went and stood beside Inman.

"If this is your idea of a negotiation then I fear you have started from a position of weakness," Bart said to Carl after noting the gun that Inman had trained on him.

"I wasn't expecting him to show up so early," Carl said.

"Doesn't appear that your plan was well thought out," Bart told him.

"It doesn't matter anymore whether I live or die tonight, this thing ends either way. The choice you will be given is whether you go down with the ship or take the lifeboat I am about to offer you and the general."

Bart looked around the room and saw what Carl had done to the walls. Every wall had a large white card stuck on it with information written in foot high letters with a bold black marker pen. On the wall behind Carl the sign detailed the available DNA available from the various blood spatter evidence and pointed out the steel ring for restraining victims.

On the wall to his left was written a list of the victims' names and the dates that their bodies were found. On the wall to Carl's right was a description and list of knives and DNA that would be found in the bathroom plus a detailed technical explanation of the room's soundproofing. On the far wall was an extra-large card providing Inman's history of aliases and crimes, starting in Vietnam then America and Thailand. The spaces throughout the room were filled out with enlarged black and white surveillance photographs that didn't record anything of significance but helped provide a general atmosphere of thoroughness.

"Show and tell is it Carl?" Bart said shaking his head in sympathy for Carl's foolishness.

"Read it all Bart! You've been protecting a truly evil man."

"You can't expect me to believe all this nonsense, can you?"

"Look at him and look around you Bart," Carl told him.

Bart looked at the man beside him and then

knew it to be true.

"Is this you Tony? This animal that kills people's children is you?" Bart said staring at Inman and becoming noticeably angry.

"Shut up Bart!" the general told him loudly with a perfect North American accent. "Shut up and stay out of it. So he's sick. Big deal. He was always sick you hypocrite. I don't remember your necktie-wearing bosses ever complaining in Vietnam when we dug people's graves before we started interrogating them."

"This is different, general," Bart pleaded.

"The hell it is. He is one of us and don't you forget it. I will deal with this problem. This is not Vietnam, this is my country and I am in charge here." Then he took a long quizzical look at Carl and asked him, "What is this Hollywood crap all about?" as he waved his arm in a circle to show that he had seen the contents of the room.

"Can you make him put the gun away? Then I'll be happy to explain everything."

"Sure, you're not going anywhere." General Amnuay took the pistol from Inman's hand and placed it in his own belt. "I'll deal with this, Tony."

"Then I will begin," Carl said. "And, yes General, this is going to be a little Hollywood I'm afraid."

Carl spoke to the room as he walked around pointing out evidence detailing forty years of global murder history.

"Wars compromise morality and Inman took advantage of that fact and made the people close to him complicit without them realising it was happening. My guess is he gradually escalated his requests for help to pull you into his wickedness. Beware of people seeking advice; most of them are really looking for an accomplice. Inman has conned you both for decades and it's time you took your souls back. This may be your last chance."

Bart stared open-mouthed as Carl finished his show and tell. General Amnuay did not show any emotion apart from mild impatience.

"That's it?" Bart said, frustrated. "Appealing to the general's better nature is your plan to bring Tony Inman to justice? Jesus Christ bwoy! This is the best you can do to protect the next poor son of a bitch's daughter. I expected more from you than this. This makes you a walking dead man. How are you planning to escape?"

"I don't need an escape plan. When I'm finished I'll just walk out," Carl told him surprisingly calmly.

Bart was flustered. He wanted Inman dead and out of his life, not back out on the streets. He had a daughter, and of all the crimes he had spent a career turning a blind eye to, the sexual torture and murder of children was not something he wanted to negotiate with his conscience.

"Madness! Total goddamn madness!" Bart said shaking his head in anger and frustration.

"General!" Carl said strongly and confidently. "You find yourself in a very embarrassing predicament. I recommend you call your friends in the police and ask them to come here and arrest your hideous associate. My advice is to tell them that you are shocked to discover that your long-time associate is quite insane and that you have evidence he is Bangkok's serial killer."

General Amnuay laughed. "And why would I do that you crazy motherfucker? I don't disagree with what you say but there is honour between soldiers and that is always above everything."

"Because even though I went with the Hollywood solution, there are no microphones which means, out of respect to you, I have left you with a way out. There is no other intelligent choice at your disposal."

"What are you talking about?" For the first time, the general looked mildly concerned.

Carl continued with his show and tell. "If everybody will look at the four corners of the ceiling you will notice four small white plastic balls. They are high definition cameras and are wired straight into the heart of the Internet at an unusually high bandwidth. We have established a website that has promised to show the whole world a serial killer being arrested in real time. An Internet first I am told." Carl looked at his watch then looked back up to his audience. "According to my watch we went viral about an hour ago. The estimate from my technical people is an audience of two million including CNN, BBC and Al Jazeera. The website provides details on your friend Tony's activities and aliases plus a few exaggerations of my own." Carl pulled a face playacting at being ashamed. "I threw in some extra stuff like Victor Boyle's confession and Tony being identified by eyewitnesses bringing victims here. Sorry about that but a little poetic license was essential."

Bart smiled happily but turned away so the general wouldn't see. The general glared at Carl. Carl continued speaking.

"Now, as nobody can hear this conversation we'll all be judged by our actions. I have finished my show and tell as Bart called it and, although the global audience couldn't hear me, everything was made clear by the writing on the walls and the highly detailed information on the website. I like that, 'the writing on the walls'. Everybody can read the writing on the wall clearly, general, apart from Tony over there, but that's because his back's up against it."

Bart laughed out loud, then he covered his mouth with his hand and said, "I think you need to take this seriously General, the agency has a lot invested in you and the shirts in Langley won't expect you to blow your career for an ex agent that they thought they had seen the back of thirty years ago."

"Bart," Carl said, "if you wouldn't mind, reach out and turn on the TV on the wall beside you."

The LED television sprang to life and showed a website listing pretty much the same information that was on the walls. In the middle of the webpage was a live stream of the room where they could see themselves. At the top of the page, on the far right, was a counter that showed 1,800,000 viewers increasing constantly.

"Don't understand how it all works but there it is gentlemen. My boffins are good. This is going all over the world I'm told."

The general said nothing so Carl concluded, "I advise you to look shocked and get on one of your many communication devices to get the police here as soon as you can. This could be the end of a brilliant career or this could be your finest hour. The choice is entirely yours and your audience is waiting." Carl waved his hand theatrically in the direction of the television.

Anthony Inman stood shaking and sweating as he realised, after the decades of close friendship, what the general's decision had to be. "A million dollars if you let me leave now," he told Carl.

Carl thought for a moment. "A million dollars is not a lot of money. Not as much as it used to be. I think I will leave you with it though. You obviously need it more than I do. You must believe that you can spend it in hell otherwise you couldn't have lived the life you did. I do believe in hell you see, there must be one. Otherwise where do devils like you come from?"

"Do you know anything about the men that robbed me?"

"I know everything about the men that robbed you," Carl said smiling.

"What do you mean?"

"They were my people. I had them fly over from the Philippines. They run a bar there but always wanted to be actors. By the time you woke up in the back of the car they were already in the air on their way back to Manila. Three million dollars and some change was a lot more than I expected you to have lying around in cash, a nice surprise. All of it is safely in an offshore bank account that is under my control. By the time I've paid the boys and bought a very expensive watch I should have two million dollars left for my retirement plan. They were harmless theatrical types and they wouldn't really have hurt you. Must've been good, I wish I'd seen them scamming you. The artist Caravaggio used to threaten to boil his enemies' balls in oil when he was drunk. I never forgot that dreadful imagery."

"But everybody said you were straight. Nobody said you were a criminal. That is why we didn't suspect you were involved," Inman said looking at the general for his reaction.

"Psychopaths like you make me think like a criminal and then it just becomes a bad habit. It takes people like me to put animals like you out of our misery."

"Amnuay, you can fix this! Please, you have to get me out of this!" Inman pleaded to his old friend.

General Amnuay did not answer him. Inman stood in front of him shaking and twitching. Carl was enjoying it too much so he decided it was time to leave.

"General, you don't need me talking to the police today," Carl said. "It'll be easier for you if I leave."

"Go away!" the general barked. But as Carl moved to walk out the general stuck out his hand and stopped him. "You have two million dollars? You will deliver half to me in cash. I want a million of it."

This was what Carl had hoped would happen. For the first time that night he felt safe and confident he was going to get to walk away and have a future. He'd held out the money and General Amnuay had taken it. He had even left Carl with half of it so he obviously had no idea how much Carl would have paid. Thailand was home and he had not wanted to have to leave it. Deal done.

Bart Barrows had his lips squeezed tightly together in an attempt to suppress laughter. Anthony Inman was whimpering and tears ran down his face. He knew that without the general's protection Thailand was about to eat him alive. His game was over and there would never be another godlike day to feed his addiction. In a matter of a few minutes he had become completely powerless. This was confirmed by the general cutting himself in for half of the money as if he wasn't even there and they hadn't been in business together for almost forty years.

"It will be done, general. And should you need me to answer questions to the police or media I will answer only as you instruct me to. I'll contact your office and let your people know how to reach me."

Carl went out the door and down the stairs past the dozen men with shaved heads and heavy boots. They opened the way and let him pass, as they had not been ordered to the contrary. He left the hideous building by its front doors, rolling up the rusty metal shutter. He stepped out onto the pavement of the main road where he saw George sitting quietly in the unlit car. Carl got in.

"It's done," he told George.

"Where are we going?"

"The worst bar on Soi Cowboy, or possibly the best, depending on how you look at it."

"You think it's safe now?" George asked as the car moved forward.

"We can assume it is. We head south in the morning to let things calm down. Oh, and by the way George, thank you," Carl said as he stretched his aching back.

"Think nothing of it. Someone has to look after you," George said with a smile.

George dropped Carl at Soi Cowboy then went to dump the car. There were too many CCTV cameras around Bangkok to continue using the stolen car after the case went public. Anyway, they wouldn't need a car on the island. George had told Carl that he would go to their houses before dumping the car and pack bags for them. Carl had handed him a key and told him some things to grab for him, not that George needed a key.

Carl walked up the narrow lane that was Soi Cowboy with its over forty bars with their neon signs advertising adult Disneyland. He knew where he was going. Carl pushed through the curtains and went in.

He was well on his way to being drunk and was contemplating calling Jacqueline when a pretty young girl sat down beside him watching as he consumed glass after glass of whisky. She was naked from the waist up and her pert young breasts became the focus of Carl's attention.

"Why do you drink so much?' she asked him.

"I drink to forget," Carl said to her left breast.

"What're you trying to forget?" she asked with concern.

"I can't remember," Carl told her.

EPILOGUE

The world's *first* capture of a serial killer via live feed was passed around social media like a fuck photo in a Catholic school. Some Facebook and Twitter users commented on how staged it seemed and that two of the men in the video did not later appear in the official police statements. The biggest complaint from the conspiracy theorists was that the picture was just a little too grainy to identify the faces properly. The last thing Damien's Finns uploaded to the site was an expression of gratitude to 'Expat Watch', a fictitious organisation of anonymous undercover volunteers that allegedly assisted the Thai police in their unenviable task of investigating major foreign criminals.

Due to the very average quality of the video, CNN, BBC, and Al Jazeera only ran the story for a day. A Thai government spokesman said, 'We do not comment on home videos posted to the World Wide Web unless they contravene specific laws of the Kingdom of Thailand.' Shortly after that the story was sucked into cyberspace to float around on the sea of yesterday's news.

Mad Mike had been right as usual; Inman's arrest

made the front page of all Thailand's newspapers. When the police discovered a walk-in safe at his Las Vegas Real Estate office with shelves loaded with jars of pickled ears the story made the front page a second time. General Amnuay declared himself a hero and Carl's name was never mentioned, much to his relief. The interrogation was perfectly choreographed and Anthony Inman accepted his guilt in a windowless room at police headquarters. After that he never spoke again. The system that had protected him for so long had lined up against him and he didn't have a hope in hell.

It was in General Amnuay's best interest that Anthony Inman spent the rest of his days in a dark cell without any contact with the outside world so that was what was going to happen. His crimes carried the death penalty but foreigners never got executed in Thailand. You never know though; perhaps they would make an exception for Anthony Andrew Inman.

Carl read all of the English language papers every morning on his idyllic island beach. He held onto the money for a few weeks to make sure they weren't coming for him. When he felt reassured by the passing of time he transferred a million US dollars to his preferred Thai-Chinese moneychanger who operated from a back room on lower Sukhumvit Road. Then he contacted General Amnuay to send one of his trusted boys to collect it at his convenience. It had been a long time since Carl had a general on his payroll.

About the Author

Harlan Wolff is a private detective and has lived in Bangkok since 1977. The nature of his work has been serious crime and corporate investigation solutions. Harlan maintains a low profile in Thailand.

You can follow him on Twitter at @HarlanWolffBKK or email him at harlanwolff@hush.com